I

c

o

p

e

GAIJIN

by Jordan Okumura

#RECURRENT SERIES

Civil Coping Mechanisms

Praise for *Gaijin*:

"And what is the measure of self inside grief? Jordan Okumura's novel *Gaijin* is a body song. By weaving stories of loss and myth, Okumura brings an identity to life, half real, half imagined. I was mesmerized from start to finish."
—Lidia Yuknavitch, author of T*he Small Backs of Children* and *Dora: A Headcase*

"Labile, alluvial, fricative, abrasive, *Gaijin* cuts a channel through stone which takes the shape of its own persistence. I *want to say your name with a rock beneath my tongue.* It stages and restages memory to pinpoint the exact site where the skin broke and the shard sank in, then gestures towards a moment-after wherein this wound, inverted, might become both shield and sword. A nervy, unnerving book."
—Joyelle McSweeney, Professor, University of Notre Dame, author of *Dead Youth, Or, The Leaks*

"*Gaijin* makes possible the impossible language of trauma."
— Molly Gaudry, Yale Writers' Conference, author *We Take Me Apart*

The narrator of Jordan Okumura's haunting and evocative *Gaijin* says, "I "want to live the life of tongues." But what if that tongue has been inscribed with the language of others? In lyric prose born of breath and body, Okumura wrestles with questions like: How to find one's self when "memories don't know how to stay past?" How to "reconcile the possibility of a girl and men" when those men have stolen all possibility from the girl? How to escape the legacy of a father when that father "is me. Wrapped in the stone of me?" In doing so, she gives us a beautifully fractured story of a journey to uncover the history of a woman hidden within the history of a family. I dare you not to fall under Okumura's spell."
—Peter Grandbois, Associate Professor of English, Denison University, author of *Nahoonkara*

"To pirate, to scratch. To press or be pressed: "into the girl corner." To watch: "the water run home." How the cliffs "ignite." Jordan Okumura's *Gaijin* is an extraordinary book of poetry written, or so it feels, into the axial space of memory, embodiment and dream. In it, a grandfather, a man "born from tears and war," moves from space to space, just as the narrator does: the "river floor," the garage that becomes a Japanese theater, the mouth "that is already closed." What does it mean to have had a hand in one's "own erasure"? I was very moved by Okumura's decision to make a book the site of "wet erosion," tongueless. And yet the stories pour out, "beautiful" in their "heat." Towards the question. Of what it would be. "To stop." I am honored to write in support of *Gaijin*, which takes it's place in the contemporary literatures of exile and diaspora: an index of fire and water, "original bone," and light."
—Bhanu Kapil, Naropa University and Goddard College, author of *Schizophrene*

"Reading Jordan Okumura's poetic prose will change the way you breathe and the way you move. Her prose reaches inside you, caresses the very core of who you are, and transforms what you thought you knew about love, hope, and desire in unnerving ways. Her writing does not simply remind me of the writing of Carole Maso, Helene Cixous, and Marguerite Duras; her writing extends this tradition of intimate, passionate writing that does not fear the pain of seeing into truth. *Gaijin* will awaken you to new ways for seeing and feeling. Each time I have read *Gaijin*, I have come to know something new about myself, about my own heart. It is rare for a first novel to look in such a relentless and courageous way into familial relationships and memories as does *Gaijin*."
—Doug Rice, author *Here Lies Memory* and *Between Appear and Disappear*

Grandpa, we are stones in each other's shoes.
In your house I am a pirate.
I need my skin to rupture.

ONE

I am told to be a narrow girl. Able to fit through distressed doorways. A breath through the keyhole. Pressing against white grain walls and brown paisley wallpaper, I duck into the rooms of my grandfather. He is in a box, collecting the skin of his children. He sucks at the air when fine-tuned cousins slide past his body in late September then retreat into shadows. Reflections in a diorama of dust. Grandpa still sits, above the tallest head framed in stained oak, entombed in artifacts, between photos of family wrapped in family.

When I close my eyes, Grandpa, I dream I am the little Peach Boy, his body covered in the soft flesh fruit. His eyes swimming with the brown of pit. I dream that I am wrapped in the falling language of your language.

The story Grandma read to me from the pages of Japanese books. Her fingers falling down the thin black symbols. Small animals scratching marks through the skin of the page. The body claws. The body silent.

I want to be a palette of morning light. Run red with blood, Grandpa. Eat from the small white wrists of your little Peach Boy.

Watch the water run home.

Two

I am spun in a house of laughter, muted by hands. Always moving from room to room, I follow the dimming light.

Grandpa's chair is stitched maroon, broad-shouldered, its weathered paws wearing away at the carpet and hardwood. He is still there, prophesying from the corner. When he died underneath Grandma's last prayer, 500 miles away and two streets toward the end of western land, I stole one single breath against a draft of salt and late summer heat. Tracing the cement snake along overcast cliffs dropping to suicide surfers, the corners of my mouth began to taper in. Water rapping against the residual rock, the questioning hammer of tapping fingers. These edges of wrinkled coast. If the rock gave way under my feet, it would be like falling into the sun, into pools of kerosene.

A face licking the water.

Cliffs that began to ignite.

To forget how to remember. Balance a palm on the edge of mama's rose-tinted mirror without eating the surface of these stories. Peel back the images that layer speaking. To be spoken by these men in my family would name me. Grandpa cursed women. Loved women. Tight in his hand, I was a woman dressed to the marrow in Portuguese blood and Japanese vein.

These wounds will open for the wrong things, child. Sitting in the corner on a pile of Bibles and dust, this child stutters a moment before speech. When Grandpa said mouth he pointed at the fixtures that made me a woman. Born into a house of mirrors.

Would you be this other man, let loose the words into the heavy fog? Would we wrap ourselves in the body of the same flag?

Polish our lives with the tongues of our children. You began all this writing so many years ago, inverted words under my skin. In a trance, you become my reflection. Swallowing your shards, these seams ruptured and fell open like the noise in your voice, stitching tales into my story.

Away.

I am told I am of the Father. Fathers. Reaped from the ash of untended graves. I sit close to the edge of the uneven grass. With the wind spitting such heavy gusts, I cannot open my eyes to see that this grass has grown over all of the names.

I want to remember our stories, Grandpa, to fill this emptying.
The beginning of memory.

In a room I find a match. We light it, Grandpa. The flame has an obese belly, arms reaching back to stir the water.

Little girls fit better in corners.

The church created shadows for Grandpa's body. Housed a cliché of his new America. He watched the church extend from the sky down. A mound of wood planks and stained glass crucifixion. Pinned. Arms open, in death. Sky breaking like the blue of shallow water. And tears. Lost words on lost men who whispered tales about Jonah. Men who read the backs of hands and the tops of heads.

The church stood at the end of all roads. Laid bare, housing dust and stories and other people's faith. The church faced west, hunched against the history of our clouded sunset, rimmed in flowers that bowed their heads back to the earth. Losing color.

Being Japanese, post-World War II, meant they couldn't even whisper their secrets. Desires. I've seen the letters from the family. Allegiance wet with ink where they scrolled their bodies into American refuge. I dream that I am born from a letter and a son, looking to be whiter than white faces painted on our Kabuki masks.

Our family, like the flowers rooted against the church, had grown into straw and pale versions of themselves, bending back towards the soil. Drunk with thirst. The church door- way warped beneath black shadows, hiding quiet conversa- tions. Endless corners of things we could not see. Grandpa reached out against the rain and felt for his son, but found only his own palms pressing water from the air. Two sons and two daughters sent out in the world. To make the world seem right.

Trace your steeple, Grandpa,
your hands that hinge towards Heaven.
In the nick of time.

Webs hung low where the walls touched the roof of God's entrance, flies trapped in foreign shrouds drenched the dark and the dreamed. Their bodies visible in small black specks. Stiff legs bent in prayer. Last dying wish. Religion in flies.

I molded hands into fists tight with tremors and clenched the torso of the church. The planks of wood held dying, their skeleton rippled with age. I felt no age before words, just splitting wood and the callous backs of banisters. I learned to back away from the field of light ignited in the doorway. The church lost its edges, became the night, opened a gaping mouth bordered by cradled insects and slender men dressed in black.

I slept with Grandpa's words.

His looping penmanship wrapping around our little naked bodies. When Grandpa dictated the letters onto Grandma's pressed flower cards, our bodies turned to petal. The ink burned, like it always did, through the sheets and the fibers of baby blue duvets and beneath beds where I littered the cards. They crept up from my childhood hiding places. Settled like dry leaves on water, always drifting just on the surface.

Grandma pushed the flower faces against the contact paper. Twelve inch voices filled the room with childhood stories. My girl cousins and I so nervous to speak over phone lines, we rippled with the family heat. Clenched hands placing only stencils of truth into letters we sent to each other down windmill roads and hiding places in the earth. Turned our bodies into animals.
Lifted our names into whisper.

God's hand is pressed against your back. With love...

Under the mattress squeezed between magazine cut-outs and tightly bound photographs, the cards pressed flat and hard into the beams. The ink bleeding south. Threads and maroon fiber stuck on the matted point of the licked envelopes, residue of tears distorted on the tongue. Feet that still drag in the houses of our fathers. The language of Japanese

internees branded the air long before this building of my
father's name. Grandpa moved under American stars. Stripes.
Even while they set fire to the tails of his name. The calligraphy. He was a symbol once. An image of a forest dark-
lined, and shaped, into a historical fingerprint. The soul
surviving in a place without language. Three palms pressed
out towards the setting sun.

When he began loitering outside of his skin, the image of
my desire began to refocus through the sins
of the Father.

I wanted to materialize the undressed cut toward bone. In
pen and ink and blood I marked my body to shroud this
nakedness while our namesakes shuddered. *Twisted girl,*
you cannot write over your skin. Don't do it in blood. I let the ink
in. All the way to my veins. Let the needle point ride the
whip of my spine 'til the symbols stared back at the shadow
generation. *You are a shadow of your country.* Tattoo number
seven. The only one I would not scratch into my geography
of scars. The only one I want now. This now. Only lasting
until this mouth has trailed off into other moments. Where
photographs twist in my memory. Grandma and Grandpa
separated by death. I wish these memories would erase
themselves and simply become stories.

I miss you. Miss you so much. I'd eat your ashes. Hold
them inside the pit of my Japanese tongue. You own my
skin, Grandpa, the one rich with Portuguese blood. Un-
nameable. When you wrote your family after this country
denied you, I became your threatening woman.
Half-haunted, half-here.

Grandpa's words erode skin over the head of a rambling
father. A son. Ventriloquist smiling. His veins reeling out

beneath his fingertips. Attached at the ribs of his children. Grandpa, a sheer thin voice over background pictures. Family sewn under my skin. He tracks his redemption in movement through our dreams, that I would give him back the tender meat of our tales. Grandma twisting her darning needles. Chewing the finer threads of skin that Grandpa had left to the women.

When Grandpa's skin began to sag back towards the earth I tried not to believe that the cancer was karma. He was denied. Then he denied the skin of his children. His body whipped the air with spirals. Sparse white hair caught in the currents. The stool pushing skywards beneath his body. Protruding legs, spreading out beneath his oversized t-shirt. Undersized body. Rose light and beige cotton blend. Stretched at the neck exposing the dark brown moles rising from his skin. The cancer ate away at his blood and tissue.

He lay in bed most days. The oak of his skin, the constellations of round stone moles, like wet wood submerged in river water. The bed cradling his body, hoisting it up off the ground where he no longer walked without help. His eyes were marble, the clouded gray inside them swallowing light. His eyelashes came together in clumps, thickening the rims of his eyes. He was crying and sweating all day. Profuse with water in our arid house. His flesh spotted with bruises, distorted plumbs against the swath of his skin. His shortness of breath buckled in his chest. Deep murmurs from an animal lost in the belly of caves. Grandpa moved his eyes when the house moved. Doors opening and shutting. Family escaping the medicated calm. He was tucked tight in his cocoon. The bed mummified him, our tears wetting the cloth that wrapped around his shrouded body.

His words became wet weather. Homage to a story created in the light of loss.

Grandma mouthed verses even when Grandpa slept. The currents in his damp pools of sight flowing downward. She read the scriptures to the room, collected dried flowers and delivered Grandpa unto death. The sounds in his gut stirred mine. The more he died, the more I marked myself into symbols. I could not find a true way to tell him I loved him. I could not tell him that the more he died, the more blood rose to the surface of my skin.

On his wall I am a fly, rubbing my black wisp legs together.

I eat from the dribble he leaves leaking down the crest of his blanket.

I stood before his ashes. Out of the dry leaves of his body, I tapped the box to see if it moved. Splintered a mouth and gave voice to this burning. His skin is still dying as the ash breaks down from rubble into dust. The Bibles that clean the house remain. Astringent and beautiful. Pages that flutter sideways. Dog-eared and creased to loop around fingers, into mouths. Bindings that tunnel air into currents that whisper. I smiled to silence. Common thank-yous under the pulse of the family breathing. I cannot forget the verse, John 3:16. It was my first reported memory. My first act for God, I could hear him say. Create. I was the will of dreams, waking through Grandpa's children.

For God
So loved
The world.

The words sounded like home. The intensity of fingers penetrating memory from leather rectangles. Black vaults of shame. Bible talk. But it sounded so familiar to me. Resonated from the throats of the men that I knew.

Three points of the body. He sits at the window. Rocking. Doesn't he. Grandpa, he is a no man's land. With one eye fixed on me he presses silence against the top of my head, even in death. Grandpa, my beloved. His memory is a famished eye, scarred with skin, sewn together at ancient seams. Out of the corner of his drooping mouth he wipes the ink that curdles into pools inside his palms. Grandpa is a vibration away from spilling over
into everything.

Inside my father is missing. Grandpa has fed him paper that lacerates.

I just want to stay quiet. Not utter another word. I want to say your name with a rock beneath my tongue.

When you hear me say it you will know what your name sounds like grinding against stones, Grandpa tells me in dreams.

For each word, I want to put shattered glass between my teeth, fallen hair, water, fingers in my mouth. When the uttering erupts, will it sound like our skin? I want the easy way out, the one that lets me slice open the mouths of my body. I want to live the life of tongues. When I crawled out from beneath your fingernails, the filth turned my skin to ash. On the shaking ground my body split into your gaping mouth.

The comfort of cold steel. I scratched my zigzag thoughts into skin. Then the break of blood. The skin exhaling, blood breathing. The cloud of white as eyes read back. Rewrite. Erasure. Blood writing words on the hardwood floor. I could smell my blood living. My mother's pin cushion stolen every night for the sake of skin-writing, memories that weren't mine. Mine now.

I search into skin and bone for words. I am too clumsy. Too impatient, I dig with a ferocity for what I used to know. I eat the words in a fashion of force-feeding. The manner of hands scooping and shoving, of pelvic bones moving touch around in my body, threads of my own clothes rubbed like flint against my skin 'til they sparked. Fire and a third generation burns, still singeing the meat below the skin.

I swallow my own blood.
I begin to lose color.
When I was a child my skin peeled back and let in the whole wide world.

EROSION

I was born with my father's story. I polish memories away.
Edges sore under the collapse of remembering. The words
were broken apart into bread, war rattled against them until
they fell from Grandpa's fingertips. Words written against
the stomach of small girls seething. From the hollow of my
navel, I wish for life to spiral out and form letters of bone
and birth. Cursive limbs that look like a girl scented with
the in-between.

Speaking tongues, language left out of the Asian fire.

I reach my fingers down. Towards the words. Nails clawing,
the scratching becoming whispers. Inscribed body binding.
Callused skin speaking against wet vein.

I was designed in the mirror of my father's erosion. Our
words are syncopated at the joint. We lose the I retreating
within us. We clamor for the dead rock winding its way
down our throats. He swallows while I choke on the stones
of our fathers.

My father studied a map of our family under the bandage
of white light that shielded him from shadow. Kicked the
table with his hands jabbing at words. Across the grain,
across the maple brown hardwood. I felt his matter moving.
The tip of his pen shifted the air. Across the city he double
clicked his pen every time his teeth found his tongue. My
father touched the vertical scar behind his ear as it wrapped
around a small section of his head. Still swelling with fluid.
I felt the words he tried to write in place of a story about us.
He wrote in my brother's name to mark the man who will
decide his fate if he does not wake from another surgery.

I am a man-made canvas girl.
Botched at the beginning of all of my father's stories.
We are a collision.   You and I.

My father used to yell at me over my desire for sounds,
votive of speech. His lips dried to gray as he spoke. Gusts
through the seams of his mouth. His words were beautiful. *Hate. Selfish. Loss. Daughter. Un-Daughter.* He is always the
incision directed at the bone. Realizing as I curved my hand
right, tilted my neck to allow more movement through my
arm, better reach with the dulling pencil, that words hurt to
write, begged the body for more with each word. Each eye
laced with lettering. I delivered lead scrapings to the page.
Wanted to write out all the secrets. Feed the paper.

My father and I sat on the couch. The light didn't warm
our backs, but spread shadow. We reach for each other over
the back of my grandfather. Our bodies buckle on the torn
page between us.

Dad's skin is olive and browning over time. He has tan
lines you would never know about. Lines from golf socks,
Nike t-shirts that are sewn symmetrically by small girl
hands. Tailoring the language into his body. Curving from
hairless bicep to soft, strong knuckles. The shorts always hit
just above the knee, at a small crease of skin that looks like
the frown on his brow. Several lines of equidistance deepen
on his forehead, stretching more and more horizontally as
the sun sets on his face. Age writes its worries along desig-
nated lines. His arms and legs form animate boundaries.

He is also missing lines.

I looked for the slight peek of yellow or peach from his ring finger. I must have created it all these years, because when I ask my mother where the white rings of flesh around their fingers have gone, she tells me that my father and her never had wedding rings.

Grandpa put his children to work fixing their legs together at the knees. Skinning them with his new language. He dug the words out of the mutton served in WWII relocation camps. Told his children stories before there were children to tell them to. Whispered them through the sheets that hung in Tule Lake, to divide the barracks into rooms.
I sold my grand piano for five dollars.
We didn't know any better.
We didn't know better.

When my father was a boy he did not get the shoes he wanted. Flagg Brothers, pointed black shoes. Back in the day, he says. Worn casually with spiked slacks. Billy Joel sings about those shoes, my father uttered to me. Sometimes he spoke softly to me. Told me about how he pared down his Japanese habits, traveled the circuits with high school animals. My father wanted to walk like them, drag and click his heels in the hallway. His never-ending desire for those shoes. He began to thread the air with the shoe laces he didn't have, to thread the shoes he did not own. This wanting. The gray in-between that found his flesh and ripped it into neutral. But his tears didn't begin to form until years later. 'Til after his daughter was born.

When he left the single-story of our family home where my brother and I grew up, he clipped our wings. A pile of primary flight feathers, teaching us in a roundabout way that our wings wouldn't work. *Don't, if you can, rely on them.*

He spoke into my mother's dreams. Left stories for me
embedded in the green carpet fibers. Creating memories of
peacetime during late summer afternoons, I could almost
remember a time when there was enough quiet to betray
the myths he left me. In the sound of night he murmured
shreds of guilt through the screen of our bedroom windows.
Was never him. He pressed his praises down my throat,
followed by the deaths he had not died yet. These dreams
I ate with fingertips. I mapped the insides of my tattered
wanting. Even in the tricks of sleep there is a grain of truth.
Sometimes like sand in the sheets they become the
sediment of my skin. Too far from water.

This isn't about my father. It is always about my father.
About the flesh I ate out of his hands as he pulled me
back from the erected crater of his father's Hiroshima. In
dreams, Grandma remained quiet on the corner of her
family's farm in Japan. Tucking dreams of ink stained teeth,
and manjū into the folds of her apron.

You will carry all your sorrows, Child. In the womb of your father.

I am at last a concubine   of your language, Grandpa.

Try not to be heard. Water is best for muted bodies pressed into girl corners. The universal solvent of muscle, bone and breath. I mimicked them as I moved around the south end of the house. There was a time for music and there was a time for crawling in dark rooms to create vacancy. Not refuge, but something less terrifying than all of us being in the same room together. I can not remember what is real, spinning in the middle of the living room bandaged in "Crimson and Clover" or trying to escape the blackness, the lightless, hot silence of the spaces that were used to scold my brother and me.

Fear of the dark.
Little wing battering the window, that could break towards air at any moment.

Now I don't hardly know her
But I think I could love her
Crimson and clover

Chords that cut and cauterized. All these things began to turn into the edges of dreams. The candles burning upside down, destroying us.

The eating of my tongue to find a way of speaking.
I have been lost.
For all this time.

PHANTOM

I dream sometimes, of being a young boy in a worn, tan
leather jacket. There has always been a distinct mirror in
these dreams. Sitting above a blue tile floor, tall rectangle
rounded at the edges, deteriorating from the constant heat
and moisture in the air. I can never see my face. Laws of
reflection.

I travel to places without mirrors, just small faces escaping
the necks of brown robes, slow boats, war, and moon cakes.
The children were my mirror. They came towards my face
like a moth flickering in twilight, hiding their stories inside
a small batting eye. So much twilight the bodyboy dissipated
into the matter of the Mekong. The earth torn open to the
slick bone.

Laos sending the evening drum beats, soft along the river
floor. Onto the belly of small boys, written in shrapnel.
His skin braised by the sun. He sat soaked in the afternoon
storm. Rolled in the grass. I listened to the water run over
the rocks in the Mekong. Piles of arms and piles of legs in
the river, trickling with the building wind.

He roughed his hands under the faucet, clenched the spigot
in his raw curl. The lid of his lips fanning wide and long.
When he looked at me I saw my hunger in his appetite,
for thin red prayer threads and pennies lost in the dirt.
The precious metal under the palm of his hand, the face of
the coin pressed between his lips, toward sinew and vein.
He lifted saccharine pools out of the ribs of his teeth and
crawled toward me, dragging the stump of his leg. The
shrapnel everywhere deep. The scar opening even then.
Ever-opening. He scratched the ground near his phantom

limb. His nails thick with mud making. He tucked the sounds of his coughing into the neck of his shirt and when he looked back at me the watching was gone. The myth of the mirror was gone.

He touched my bracelet, small wood beads leaving divots in my wrist. The boy turned away and back into twilight, pulling deeper into the ground.
Baby boy.

The Sunday paper is wrapped tight. Plagued by jean and corduroy. Little children rivets. The rubber band still stretched and screaming. The bed whimpers as I wrap into my self. White planks of wood. The lights go out and the bulbs are loosened. Space invades skin. Sparks and electric currents shutter to sleep. Will me to peace. I tug at the blue reversible blanket to cover my 10-year-old skin, that is exposed when too close to air. The canopy bed pulls away. Arms reaching up. Limbs finding cool air above the tracts of adult voices hanging around the door frames. The light crying to be turned off. I hear it. It was safe at first, illuminating the corners full of acrylic baby doll hair and holiday dresses, hems always dancing away from the matted carpet.

The body of light from the bulb has begun to fidget and hum. In the next room my father hovers inside of his suits. Beyond the call for lights-out in a house with only two children, a woman and a man, the bulb begins to murmur. The sounds of an old man hunched over his voice.

The light splices the room, projects against the window. And the room of the window. Behind the crackling voices of recorded soap operas, the whistle of a car alarm breaks the evening script. Then static.
The sides of my eyelids rupture. Binding at the lash.
To open.

At two or three o'clock in the morning, the skin between my legs would heat up from dreams. I pressed my hand to surfaces close to flesh. The scent of deep sleep, house wide, and me. Heat and fire.

Being a woman will haunt you.

A hand steeped in sweat holds heat against the lower right
corner of the window pane. Someone looking out.
Someone looking in.

Betrayal. Skin that does not hold the language of spirit soil.
Shattered against the wall by the newcomers. For the newcomers. I am surrounded. My father's house full of voices.
Sounds that stumble like sleepwalking children onto the
back of my tongue and wait for me to speak. All that weight.
My grandfather is a man born from tears and war. A trip
to a new land that changed the stigmas traced into his skin
before he was born.

The garage door collapses into a stage.
Framed in Kabuki masks.
I hold the broken body of a house.
Baby bird.

Dust collected in the creases of our white wood doorway.
Sand from our shoes stuck to the rim of the house, hair we
tugged from each other's dodging heads, rust from garden
tools that we wiped on our "daddy and me" t-shirts, salt
from our tears, skin from naps on the warm concrete in the
fall. My brother and I ran through the strands of streets
with our fingertips touching. Our ankles ached from pound-
ing the slanted sidewalks after daybreak swim meets and we
stuffed our soccer shoes with newspaper to prolong returning to the house. Hung our swimsuits on the back of plastic
patio chairs. Avoided the doorways that opened the silent
boundaries that marked our house for mouths muted from
being neither Japanese nor Portuguese.

The house was like a vacuum. In spring, my mother power washed the front of our home. The water beating in high volumes against the brick, swallowed sound and a year of storms and silence. She twisted the door off of its hinges, replaced it, painted it shades of bruised flesh and magenta. Changing it constantly in rhythm with our growing bodies. As we grew out of our hyper-colored t-shirts and Speedo bathing suits, the house would shift so that it never seemed to age. She changed small parts of the house to keep the place alive. Transplanted the orange bush with crape myrtle, the linoleum with hardwood. She sat still to sleep.

In July, my father filtered the light through summer screens. Their heavy metal stitching catching the best part of the 4 p.m. rays cooling them against the rust-colored carpet. It was a house for whispering. Twelve-inch voices, so my brother and I were always close to each other's skin. Talking deep into each shoulder blade, smelling the chlorine drying on our toweled bodies. His cheeks always shaking from the air-conditioned rooms, drying out our throats, making the acid of lemonade linger a while longer.

My father always made us keep the doors open. Bedroom doors, bathroom doors. They never moved freely in their battered door frames. The subdued movements in his house left the skin and lint to drift down in layers on the carpet. My brother and I walking along the edges of clouded hallways, kicking dust. My father gave no attention to the things that he couldn't return to their exact same resting place when he was finished using them. When he moved away from us, our torrent of breathing pushed the air and dust all around the house. The old breath in stale still corners, touched new rooms. Began to smell like gardenias sifting through open windows.

The thin seasonal screens let in the day. Rose and beige. The sunscreens enacted violence on the light, heavy cages barring the windows. My mother bent their stiff bodies from their frames, tossed them under the persimmon tree. Unsalvageable. The house that could no longer ignore the light.

But before that, the doors were always open. He removed the doors from their frames. I could hear the screws grinding together in the corners of his mouth. We all feared the sleepless night, each disappearing into the bones of the house.

His door was always closed when he was home. He paced one end of the house and my mother, the other. They moved around each other like ghosts. Or magnets turned the wrong way.

The corners of the house were always less severe at night, but opened into dreams. I could see the glare of light the TV threw against the walls. Its terminal flicker killing the quiet and stillness. The lick of light noting the changing scenes, gave just enough to pull shapes out of the darkness. Light switches needed permission to be used.

The family room was off limits. It held a pool table when my parents first bought the house and I was born. No money to buy furniture but they got a good deal on the black credenza. It turned into a picture museum when my brother and I got older. White carpet, white frames holding lifeless stories of people we didn't know. Frame fillers from Marshall's and Ross that were replaced over years with photos of Nana and Papa, Grandpa and Grandma, us at Easter. No photos of my parents together unless my brother and I were wedged between them. Our teeth floating up out of black mouths. The white room held broken bodies of furniture we could not touch, still partially housed in plastic wrapping.

When Dad left, the house began to move. Mom shifted the crown moldings, children, carpet colors, appliances, fiancés, and boyfriends. She painted walls covered in crayon and then layered them again in a shades of light that didn't quite match. The carpet that darkened from a deep rust toward a burnt orange as the sun lightened the acrylic surface. I crawled the carpet slowly before my dad moved out. Pulled myself along the fall orange fibers with tiny palms. The movement like a body traveling the rungs of a ladder.

At night the garage door rattled shut. My father had entered the house, his tie never undone until he was in his room. Changed into his warm-ups. He bent the last few hours of light before bed into avoiding our attention.

Daddy vacuuming over footprints in the white carpet, twisting his head into unhinged doorways looking for loose clothing, small corners of sheets that could be blown out of place with gusts from his mouth. The garage shut in the perfect dark spots for the bad girls and baby brothers that didn't want to tag along for the ride. In one of my father's fits he would lock us in the garage. Lights off.

Keep them off.
I'll know if your fingers are there
on the switch.

I twitched in the dark. The lines of light erased and the scent of rust was so strong I could taste it. My elbows shook like shards of un-tempered glass that violently pushed my brother away from me. He screamed until I reached for the light switch. He screamed until daddy turned on the light. I would dig my heels into the carpet. My father's ringless right hand around my wrist. He pulled my weightless body shaking in his palm. I was the broken limb he drug to the grass pile on the edge of our property. His clenched muscles, thin lines and varicose veins rippling along bone. Even in his sleep. I was tossed into the heap of dark shapes tangling the garage trappings into a solid mass when Daddy closed the door. I sat in the garage, feeling my way around pointed edges of filing cabinets, the trailer of the bass fishing boat, letting large plastic bins of sports equipment steer my body into erasure.

The closing door would drift over my line of sight.
The jutting shadow over my tiny girl torso, wings spread.

Night, baby bird.

THREE

The boy, he pushes into me. The wind scrubs the outside of the building, the room is no longer a part of the apartment complex. His room is no longer attached to the living room where my girlfriend sleeps un-waking through Jack Daniels and Stoli breaths. His skin is not soft or kissing or speaking. He is whispering all the time. He is welcomed and hated and I hold him so close to my heart that he singes the air with his heat. When I exhale, it is his breath in my lungs. I can't say the word *rape* without feeling my skin lift away from bone. The fire burns those places that make me a woman. I am left with the char of his heat on my flesh.

Both boys and all boys. They have become my folklore. In remembering I recreate and forget the violence. My violence.

I invade my body with them, these dreams of being them. In the middle of trying to find my way back to my own de-sire, I dream his. His fingerprints tagging the places on my body that he wants to remember. I feel the heat of the body parts I don't have. The phantom dreams. I am defensive and strong when I am him.

When I dream of my father, my grandfather, I become a lit-tle girl wrapped under layers of forgetting. They have roots and a tongue and they are deeper into their stories than I am. I am only floating on the surface of my myth. When I am the beautiful boy, walking effortless in and out of the night, I am forceful and demanding. I hold down my own body in dreams and struggle to force desire back between my legs. I wet my lips with this violence of being raped.

He pushes away from me, arching his voice into the corners of the ceiling. His words wrap around the room, all rooms.

I roll around the word mother in my mouth. It turns into mommy. I rape myself out of being a victim. The pity that can only be undone with rage.

When they fished my carcass out of the pool of tangled bed sheets, sweat and whispers, I see him sitting on his knees in the rectangle of street light illuminating the hollow doorway. The flashlights blinked at me. The faces of the police replaced by the white beams of light.
A woman's voice said *mother*.

I remember very little. Each year less. So I make up the fractured layers of story a little more as time passes. I become an antelope, a teenage boy with his ankles deep in the Pacific Ocean, a girl selling umbrellas in Vietnam. I am less the 18 year-old girl with her knees in the grass, less the 21-year old tom-boy draped through the rough armored hospital gown, fighting the urge to tear through any opening I can find in my skin.

You got what you deserved, they tell me.
I have always opened to the possibility of pain. Of obscuring what's right. I own the hand I have had in my own erasure.

I. My own cautionary tale against light.
Mommy this. Mommy that. Residual hands pressed their hands on my back.
Down, into slices of newly shaven goose bumps.
Still smelled like work. DS-3 cleaner.
Gin martinis.

These memories don't know how to stay
past.

Pressing against the voices of family in hallways, I begin to scratch at the river that wants to come out. Slice the cervix in half. Remove rape.

I open my hand and cover a mouth that is already closed.

FOUR

My mother is missing in memories. Ever present in dreams.

She burrows deep inside my stories, anchors the life we have lived together, holds my heart tight inside the pools of her palms. She is a whisper against the sounds that knuckles make, being dragged along the hallway walls. She was in the shadow with me.

I want so badly to be my mother's daughter, but I let Grandpa's blood write scripture on my teeth. My mother, a pool from which I drank. But for all of her wishing, I only bring her the sadness of a daughter's denial.

You drink the words of your mother, child. I write mine against your back.

I found her once, or did I dream her. Head tilted over the white porcelain toilet bowl, knees buckled towards the center of a silent, black space, her body submerged in shadows. The howling echo, a parade of blue. My mother's wet swollen face turned from a pasture into a shattered mirror. Her hands wrapped into her mouth, holding the spit from running down her chin. In the puddles on the floor I found my mother's words mangled among the hair and old footprints.

Long after my father left the house, she wandered in the spaces he had left behind for her body. Not given back to her. But discarded, that she might wipe away the sins he had left for her to carry. I draw lines on her pillowcase with my eyes. The bleeding black mascara that comes from drugstore bargain hunting. My lashes creasing at the fold of my eye to the cloth. I can't sleep on my stomach anymore. Nor on my sides. Not firm enough to support the gravity against my skin. I have one eye aware of any possibility of reflection. The other sits under my tongue trying to find speech. A shaking child between the bed sheets. Ripe flesh growing old between my legs. Mom tasting the pillowcases with her eyes. Turning the water black.

I taste the words that could not save me. Her guilt, a wet paste swallowing fingertips.

My mother lived under the rash of men. Beneath their fingernails. Reclaiming her body through the dead skin they left behind for her in pockets of air. She came from the earth, from Holsteins and thick bales of hay, rotting sweet. Her hands took shape from the backs of animals. Beasts white with milk, lining the insides of her mouth. From the womb of my father's family she sat coating her wounds with the words of a man inflicting men upon his children. My grandfather fed her my father. Taught her how to love a tyrant. Her hair whipping across her eyes, slicing away the deep mud of Point Pleasant, of Nana and Papa. Down the shallow streets of his father's lies, my mother was taught the language of my grandfather. When the whispers became too loud to create silence, she broke through the skin binding her to my father's back. When the seams of her skin broke, they made a mouth. Out of the mouth came the lies of the Father.

My mother escaped.
She slipped away from the dangling carrot that rotted in the room of my father's family. Somehow she forced my father out into the Sacramento night. Out of her breath.

I dream of holding my mother. But I can't dream her there because I have my father's hands and at times his fury. I wish her into my bones, that she will somehow find a way into my blood. Instead she pulls the tails of letters as they spin away from my body. An act of removing the lines of ink. The scent of safety. Gardenia, my favorite flower, now reminds me of those boys I tried to scrub out of my skin like dust ushered off hardwood floors, toward the stoop and out beyond the light. The breath I find at times reminds me of hot summer days dreaming under water. That peace. The silence that sings. An unlikely marriage.

She doesn't help me to understand. Only to love better.

FIVE

Thailand was stone walkways and temples etching gold into the sky. Laos was the deep movement of a country finding itself in roots, growing slowly again. Vietnam was a scream. Cambodia a whisper.

I find refuge in drifting into others' stories. Level the bone, back to the earth. Skirting the dirt-edged roads, twisting over the regions still remembering their own histories. I need to slip out of the skin of a family stitched tight together by reason and with the scars of loss, now stuccoed with smiles.

Running towards forgetting. From the friends riding the storms of their own stories. The footprints still warm on the sidewalk. From standing still too long. In my hands I held the shard of a pencil and wrote secrets onto pieces of torn skirts. Left them at the bottom of beer bottles in Chang Mai, wrapped them inside rice paper in Hội An, between the lips of a boy in Phnom Penh, against the palm of boy from Australia who kissed me in the sand in Hue.

The puzzle of images still retreating away from one another, I wanted to reconcile the possibility of a girl and men. And a name.

In Bangkok I stumbled into a paralysis. It moved into my dreams of death when I desired to wander under foreign tongues. Within them. I wanted to escape the utterances of too many fathers. The country that changed colors and movement into the canvas of my body.

I ran my fingers against the wall of a garden temple as Bangkok pulled back my skin. The stampede of bones on

the street scampered through the air and I wandered out onto the hot concrete of foreign dust. Rubber that burned the air. The lines on the signs weaved and wandered between tear drops of ink. Bashful. They clung together tight and lean. My body calcified between them. My grandfather already gone. Plummeting into his own story the same year as 9/11. A year of longing.
For breath.

Shrill bike boys tucked their hands under their face masks. Sucking air through fine threaded particles and heat. Whispered about toothless children and the border at Lao. The ladyboys skirted through the veins of the city behind red wax lips. Movement that became water and red mud creeping up through the rocks of the city. Traffic rubbing against skin, riding bone.

At home the chorus of Bible lines lulled the waking to sleep, but I rocked under the row of bells that stratified sound and bled the marrow of unkempt words.

A bell for a prayer. A bell for each ruin that returns to the earth. The sounds of stories still caught between who I was as a child and who I believe I was as a child. Still a little girl remembering. The pulse of air in drying body caverns, tasking the rage to wilt back towards blood. The steps of the temple drifted up and circled away. The building was a shard of bone, clean and smooth. I caught the last bit of a tangerine robe wrapping around the tapering wall. Mapping the rudimentary lines of the sky.

I stood with my ears in my hands. I heard the sea, now that I was landlocked. Felt the pressure of his body on my skin though he orbited the grid of dreams in midtown Sacramento, still smiled in the orange light in Cancun. Those beautiful boys, thousands of miles away but inches from my skin, where I cried like a small child before words, to keep them out of my body. I have manipulated their movements in my memory so much that each boy's face has blurred into my own. My hands are calloused from dragging weights to strengthen the muscles I should have used to push them away. Men threading their fingers through my joints, my movement arthritic from their fictions. Our fictions, that made me their man.

The bedding in Chang Mai smelled like bleach and peaches, reminded me of Nana and Papa's house on Point Pleasant. Chicken coop in drying grass, chasing lizards in the barn, wrapping my little boy body in Nana's rouge red night robe.

The sheet pulled taut over my face. Spit pooling around my tongue, three fingers against my abdomen writing in scratches as I dream. The small torn edge of the plane ticket into Bangkok tucked into the edge of literature on Thai customs. The mosquitoes buzzed and their broad rippling strokes gave the air the movement of life. The sheet moved into the yawn of my mouth filtering cries and small bodies of words manifesting on my tongue and I pressed my opening body upward into the sheet. Room filled with sleepless air.

I want my body to dream with me.

Except when his foreign hands are on my back.

Accept that his foreign hands are on my back.

Six

I look back in photographs. Always speaking. Gracing the edges of what the future could look like. I pulled myself out of the Sacramento heat, the body sustainable in the state of survival. Hunger and impossible desires. I lifted off the gridded country and drove my hands and feet deep into the foreign mud. Time becomes a canvas. I imagine the photographs riding an underlying river, wrapping my tongue in home. They carry some deeper feeling than my finger can wrestle into word. But I try time and time again. Bathing the open wound in light. Beautiful light of fathers. Lovers. The road at twilight.

Breath and the creation of space. Away from my father. He bleeds in my dreams and times his entry. I wait for the smallest gap in this story to allow him in. He does not wait for permission. Nor is he even *him* anymore. He is always present and willing in the men I love, to open directly into their words and invade their individual light.

Things I cannot forgive myself for.

He is me.
Wrapped in the stone of me.

I remember my way to dreams, waiting for the market in Bangkok to quiet down, the simmer of street grease cooling on the sidewalks. Waiting for the sky to darken and my body to smudge into the dust and movement. Distracted, I stopped existing anywhere but outside of myself. A thread that tethers me to the earth. My name scratched in spices and stitches. Always scared of the clamor my story makes. I keep stopping to get directions, over time, spreading myself thin.

Even though Grandpa is gone, he has spokes reaching out
to brace him to the world. Even in memories he is always
the voice with joints that hinge on these stories and bring
me back to the body of the Father.

Planted feet, not leaving Southeast Asia. Damp hair in
the relentless moisture, teeth stained with red mud and
Vietnamese coffee. I am drinking of my skin, and still in
all this other, I cannot sleep. I created bed folds to line
my body and felt the same detachment, the open stretch of
unoccupied space that is always there. Body or no body. Last
waking thoughts *let me sleep through the entire night.* Fleeting.
To be hung over from sleep would be joy. To have one sigh
during the day that is not medicated and suppressed. The
words that break the land, the palm, the map of my body,
leave me with all this wanting.

Body memories and blood running. Desire to find the heat
that would maneuver paralysis towards love. Be welcomed
back to water.

Instead of watching the children in Siem Reap dragging a
leg, crippled from loss of use, I could see the story inside
their scripture. Blue blood cataclysm.

Instead I hold us down for the slaughter.

MOMOTARO

I read the little Peach Boy through the reminiscences inside
my grandmother's stories. I never knew what the symbols
were trying to tell me, what the black wooden creatures
meant. I read them as bodies moving through a forest,
skeletons without their armor, tree houses erected between
warmer seasons. I read these lines outside my family's language, in order to un-name.

太 I spread out open, brittle, becoming. Change my shape,
shifting between fears and desire, my fingertips only remain
in sameness. The map of my body controlled. Grandpa, the
cartographer, trapping tight the stories of the skin.

住 The broken home pieced back together with the wires
of a ventriloquist. Fingers that blush with heavy movement.
The walls all falling down. My father was hushed, deprived
of volume and the spaces of Japanese skin. He hangs his
body, a tent against the noon sky. He sweats and coats the
air in steam.

草 The hang men in the family are the same color. They
stand themselves upright. Swinging their bodies against the
pitch of the wind.

の We broke out of wonder, our bodies in the middle of a
healing spell, were broken again. My grandfather told me, I
am not still enough to surrender. Not the stillness of reflection or the moment of hands. But the kind that is like a
broken mouth. All these broken mouths.
Broken mouth.

意 You are a paradigm of shapes he says, he points to the oval of my face and the slits in my body. Open wider, he says. She loses flight, falls toward the drought, the ground writing her name in splintering bone.

The symbols open like a leaflet of what can exist. These myths holding the family together. Small children with limbs lifting away. Bound to the un-living of their stories.

Already a fragment,

already a fragment.

SEVEN

The family is like one body. Moving against the sides of bone teeth. A red sheet with the bodies of the family rolling beneath it. Grandpa with the scorching lips of atomic bombs closing tight on the bellies of words too close to the edge of skin.
To breathe.

When the first words began to stir beneath their skin there was wet erosion. These exhalations.

I am born from a bomb Grandma says

skin speaking

it severed me from the family by deleting the edges that spell out our wet

wooded name

receive

and I reach out with the black hand of a black sheep

undo the seams that cover this tearing

stitches of whitespace in the absence of ash

turn these stories into spools of Grandma's yarn

to release the child into the burning body

twist the stories from my throat and Grandma reaches

with her pin cushion

belly bulging into the fire of her children

covers their mouths from speaking

out of the quaking stone of a city silenced before bodies burnt into symbols

Grandma lost her tongue

mimicked the shadows swallowed by the rape of a bomb

standing behind the ash falling from her hair she doles out the bones that
buried her skin into clean white mouths
twisting the long strands of stories from her knitting hamper
Grandma feeds me the pages of her story
to swallow
she says that our fingers are keeping score
driving blood back in to the prison of her body
the heat buried in my lungs
you say I am the fixings of my mother's womb
in the ash covering your skinwords
I move my bones into the thread,
press my body against stones 'til it speaks
of dust

Under the instruction of my grandfather, Grandma rinsed her shears to garnish the wages she would give to my grandfather after my father was born. In his womb, my grandmother stitched the umbilical chord into the form of a small girl. With her shears she removed the chord of flesh and darned the skin back together. The small girl began to grow in the image of her father.

The night begins to fray, becomes two shades of family that my grandmother could not name. In the part of the night that was her womb, she moved her legs. Scissored them towards the valley. Her movement made her skin tear towards her heart. She descended into the scarred city, the sound grooves, cement stitching and the veins of the city break into gray friction and the tread of the family, dragging its feet.

The smell of my grandmother's yarn spinning from dust between her legs. The land cut off the sky as her face fell into water. Dreams.
Run your hands along the city. Stone fruit falling to retreating ground. Your skin is under. Here.

I want to break words with you. Roll them like worn glass between our hands. Graze the outsides of our mouth with sand dripping from paper.
Swallow the scent of water, running over. Washing clean our backs.

The wet drew my father's eyes to the ground in the city. The Japanese herded into American men. Trials on his skin as he tried to pull the last of his blood from the stones of the house.

When my skin holds its breath, pigment begins to morph. Blood rushes towards the center of eyes. To fingertips. Bandit knuckles beat holes through white paper. White walls. I run with hands clasped in prayer against the backs of pews beneath the tip of an old Baptist church. 'Til friction turns to liquid fire and Grandma wrenches her knotted paws into her purse and pulls out the plastic bag of candy she has had for grand-children-years. Grinding lead against the embossed red leather bindings 'til they gave way to thread and stitch.

We three harnessed hot to the page. The girl cousins, the unnamed trinity. Always digging our fingers into existing. Burning still, the embers stoked for being ghosts, tipping stories into fire. We leave submissions at the door. Rings of light housed in shadow. Accessing nothing but our bodies. Using words like tunnels, to move from one place to another. To be allowed to write the way a tunnel uses light. To burrow deep, to crave corners filled deep with myths about us. We three, wrung deep with the torture of silence, our small hands lit with the abandon of our blood. It leaves us caught in drought, wrung dry to heal, wrung dark without light.

We three, the girls, the wounded.
We are your Eve, Grandpa.

Page burning, page reflecting the lack in our bodies. The little girls bathing in a page, running our fingers over each other's lips.
    In want of water.

Hold deep, the Bible tells the little girls, hold deep the silence locked in skin and bone. Be the woman racked with the torn edges of scripture. Grandpa hid Bibles scented with his speech, under our beds as we slept.

    Bring down the pencil to paper   and push through.

EIGHT

I pulled the silk around me in Vietnam. So close to being
breakable, to tear through it with my teeth. Enormous
gasping holes for my body to slide through. Open up the
hinges of my legs, my arms, breath underneath. Beneath
them. The shop open at each wall. The small courtyards of
stones twisted from their original lines of placement. The
room was full of warm air lifting the corners on cotton, silk,
linen. Squares stacked to the ceiling. I was adopted into the
heat and scent of something moving. The dreams of patterns
I had in Hoi An were like water returning home.

Clothes are sacred to me because they carry inside them
all the scarred scorn of a body against itself. In the stitched
hems I still feel invaded. The layers can be penetrated.
Pores open and spill scent out of crescent button holes and
partially tailored lines. I feel the cross hairs move with the
breath of others. Another's hands building my body from
scraps on the floor. There have been other's hands in my
clothes and I dream of this. But I dream of hands that hold
carefully, with palms catching and not pushing away.

These other hands that have always haunted my clothes,
hands and machines. Living in the scorched skin of a costume.

The girl fluttered around me, opened her arms and spread
a ruler across my body, writing my figure into numbers
on the piece of cloth she had torn from a miscalculated
skirt. She looked like a dancer, the way she bent at the hip.
Her body glided up and down the length of my limbs. She
pulled my arms away from my body and turned my palms
toward the rafters. I wanted her chin in my palm, her thin
stalk-like fingers around my waist. I wanted her to keep
humming, teach me her dance.

I forced myself into her palms by pulling the fabric tight around my torso, my belly, the small budding hill against the embankment of my rib cage. She frayed the thread with her teeth, wet the fabric with her lips, whispered her secrets into the double stitch. She was so close. I wanted her to taste me. Tell me I was really there. In this now. That the water I heard running in the side room was real. Slip a wet finger into the arm of my jacket and run it around my wrist, put the pad of my finger against the middle of her tongue. Feel the life there.

I move my hands around other people's hands. Scars. Metal shards that bend to bind my body in. Her lips, all day, with the thread of my body between them.

She stood behind me in front of the mirror and asked me if I liked it. I said yes, very much. She pulled at the center of my back and said she thought I looked like a girl in a man's coat. Should she take out a pleat? Make a second row of buttons for something more fitted. She traced the outline of where my body should have been and laid a piece of green silk across my shoulder. Poked at my lower back. When I laughed, her eyes lengthened into a smile over the green swath of silk. The emerald ripples, whipping tails of thread.

She said it would be ready in three days and called for a boy on a motorbike to take me back to my hotel. But I told her I would walk. Pressed the soles of my new sandals with the impression of my feet. She did not understand most of what my English was telling her. She handed me a narrow yellow receipt and turned toward the frame of an open wall, waved at a man in beige linen. The breeze opened up the still pockets of air in his clothes and he looked like he was floating.

I dream of Grandpa without his belt pulled so tight.
And my father without his face pulled so tight.

The sacredness of clothes opens the places for another country. Carries inside them the gray, the rocks underwater, the
little peach boy, the saturated body. I force myself into
another's hands, two continents away breathing under the
sallow light between rolls of linen, corduroy, her burlap,
she is piecing together my skin. Places where she frayed the
thread with her teeth, wet the fabric with her tongue, whispered her secrets into the double-stitched lining that speaks
desire against my legs. Calluses and scars, shards and lips.
Telling their stories over the top of the knitted girl.

Under orange light Grandpa wades through blankets. *Try
these tasks of stone. Fight light with corners.*

The dream goes unpunished in the waking and I eat the
body of men with hands ravenous and hard, built with bur-
dens slight with touch. The lack of feeling dries my tongue
and I kiss boys with the skin of Grandpa's leather belt.

He snaps it wildly in the air. The buckle loose, breathing
now after the skin of his waist has lost its shape. Never
touching us, he chases us from door to door, herding us
through each opening until he has poked and prodded without slapping, touched each desire in us to speak. Speaking
in order to disobey his stacks of words in the teeth of his
books. He is fingers and lengths of leather. He is beautiful
in his heat.

NINE

There is a scent that changes everything. In the residue
of clothes, water rushes through. The streams turn from
this skin. The soul pinches the eyes closed. I smelled you
once, the writing that brought me this close to your skin,
also brought your scent, Grandpa. When I closed my eyes,
memory staged a Sunday afternoon. You would not keep
your words concealed. They wanted to tear away at our
beginnings, the way the sky tears apart cloud cover over
the ocean. The need to dissipate more than reveal, to make
room for memory.

You never pause when you speak. Even when you are so
close to death. Words written on the insides of your palms.
Always remembering what you have written. I am tethered
so close to your words.

The family gathered. Grandma's belted dress rippling
around her in waves like floral flames. Grandpa slid in sideways in the passenger seat. Crumpled against the gray up-
holstery. His head nodding against the overcast sky. Animal
clouds bulging against the wind. A tired trucker dragged his
feet over the church sidewalk.

The silence before we tried to bring your skin suit inside
the church. Your memories waiting for you. People who
wanted to see you were dying.

Grandpa packed into the car, and I squeezed in beside him.
Pushed my bottom towards his feet and sat against the foot
panel solidifying a cradle beneath him. Fish bowl eyes,
splintered at the corner and speaking.

Will I accept God.   I told you that I would. Would
I lower my face under God's pools of forgiveness.
                    I told you I would see you again someday soon.

I want to wear you. To have you fit me like a weathered
shirt, want so badly for our buttons to align.

In the sheets of the linen that hold him he is a newborn
baby. Flossed of all his fears and rubbed clean. In my
dreams he is karma and redemption. In my dreams, Grandpa is someone else. To believe in it now. As a now that will
forever be past but that will always stain my forward moment. This belief that crossed our eyes out. The Cross. That
made our mouths bleed tears.

Collectively, we have these thoughts, the girls in my family.
Always made to be girls and not women. They tried and are
trying still. About metal yard sticks and a forbidding grandfather screaming. He is several and always the same. All
and nothing, the spirit of our fingertips touching. Without
his movement, we were just voices in rooms. Our bodies
that had not been molded yet from his apocalyptic mouth.

My cousin and I sat with our legs stretched out in front of
our small narrow bodies. Perched on a brown futon. The
hall light glazed over with dust, the porcelain shade had
a belly of painted pink flowers. When we whispered only
the air between us moved. Children scampered around our
bodies and we became silently aware of our breath, the
blood moving under the heels pressed, palm beating, of my
grandfather's swollen wrists. He has been writhing too long
in his skin.

We were pinned to our bodies. Clothes that mended our tears in the parchment of Grandpa's calligraphy. Maybe he has always known that the skin he stitched for his family would never fit. He laced the womb with wet pools of stories that began to shift towards his wandering children.

In photographs, memories alter.
Are altered by a body searching for understanding.
I am. Taking a picture of these pictures, in the same skin that shares stories between women losing women in my family. My body is a negative. Original memories that have been tampered with. In my eyes, I am already searching for the beginning. The frequency of light that tastes like the desert, tastes like the desire for something blue, the myths swallowed in wet mud, the sound of a child descending. Changed in the instant they were photographed. Memory of light and time. The slice of life emerged and open. I was born a girl. The act of a mother walking through Florin Mall, begging me to come. The water that slowly broke after laps past barred jewelry store windows, the Orange Julius counter in fluorescent light, automatic glass doors leading to new toasters and hand towels. Promises.

Dad frozen in the pictures.
New position for a son turned father. The man I forever needed to be in order to disappear out of this skin.
Stones grinding even now.
The skin rubbed away at the edges and my father whispering to an unnamed baby girl.

We are what the rigid call by our American names. The cousins rigid with shadow. We blend like gardenia into air, tipped off by the movement of men in the rooms we would like to call our own. They eat our hands and our feet and

their smiles are beautiful and their teeth are thick and rug-
ged like Grandpa's parchment. From mouths being closed
so long
so long
so long.

Deep inside the wood room we learn to forget where we
came from, the stories that slid from my mother to me over
wet walls of skin holding tight, the dreams of children. I
denied the passing on of my stories on, and my body now
devours, finds the soul still sitting opposite the range of my
touch. Somewhere, that I can only get to, by forgetting and
forgiving.

TEN

The thunder was soft. Torrential rain fusing with the sound of bare skin on an aged soccer ball, lifting again and again off the tops of little boys' feet. They crowded together in the dirt lot across the road from where I stood at the café, waiting for the sky to rest its erupting. The handle of the storm steady above my head. The brown tile floors absorbed the light, washing water against the blue walls that raised out of the dirt surroundings. The sun still glowed behind the wet clouds bulging over Bokeo. My session timed out on the old, lumbering computer hunching on one of four tabletops.

I stood inside the glass door and watched the street turn to pools of rust, the boys letting it cover their feet with the viscosity of warm wax. The girl who had taken my money for the computer held up a cup of tea under her nose and smiled at me. I wish I had a picture of that moment. The deep trust in her eyes. She handed me the tea and pointed to an umbrella propped up against the wall in the corner near the two glass front doors. She put it in my hand and I took it. Imagined a blinding blue umbrella against the heavy gray sky.

I watched the boys slice the road with laughter, drench themselves in joy in the passing storm. The girl spoke no English, but gestured toward the road. I knew that she could not give me the umbrella. I knew that I would hold her hand if I could, just to remind myself that touch could be as simple and sublime as a passing hand shake. She knew I would bring it back, even if I did not know if I would.

Somewhere in this world, at the base of a temple, along a muddy road that bled into the river, the kind, trusting heart still waits for the chance to dream someone's heart intact. I wanted to kiss her on the back of her rippling dark veined hands.

I want to stop being the wounded wounding.

I walked out into the rain, tiptoed down the clay steps buoying up fractured turquoise tile. I held the umbrella by its crooked tail and let the rain spread over my face before opening its blue belly and raising it to the sky. I slid with short steps through the vein of mud and gravel. Wrapped through its walls of small hut shops and let the water soak up into the thin cotton pants that sealed my body in the wet gray light. The rain danced on the rising wind, lifted the umbrella up and down in my grip. I loosened muscles in my fingers and let the umbrella fall away from the sky. The water pooled in the shallow dips of my collar bones.

I listened to the monks chanting. Their words spilling down the blue slough of steps and burrowing their bodies in my ripe brown skin. The sky gleaning away the bones I knew were buried everywhere in this country, rinsing clean the old myths.

When I close my eyes, Grandpa,
I begin to dream.

ELEVEN

Grandpa never offered me anything with his hands. He
placed an apple on the table in the circle of light dropping
down from a glass and gold-rimmed lamp slightly swaying
over our heads. He avoided my palm. My eyes.

For my father, his brother and two sisters, it was a carrot. He
dangled it in front of their faces to teach them hunger. Sliced
it into thin orange coins and placed in on their tongues.
Over their eyes. He raised it just out of reach of the children's hands. Nails cut close to skin, scraping at the air.
Mouths wet with the want of carrot. When they could not
reach the carrot, they stood on the backs of their children
and craned toward the light. Children on the backs of their
children. We covered our faces to hide us from the brightness.
We breathe the breath caught between the mask and our faces.

We are profane in our inversion of tradition, Grandpa whispers.
His death is my hiatus.

I should never have stopped my infant movements across
the floor by hands and knees. This closeness to the ground.
The earth receiving my handprints. I reached the rim of the
house where Grandpa reinvented history, cut my hands on
the glass windows. *Always knew there were never any doors for her.
Because she was a girl. She was a child that never spoke.* The murmur of insects seeps through the shattered glass. I am a girl
rooted between letters and censored out of the body of his
ancient language. Grandpa tore from the single symbol of
our name, a string. Bound it around the tongues of the girls
in my family. Tethered the boys with a tale of sounds. The
broken language slipped into veins to burn their memories
of all this chaos.

Half inside the house, wounds were leaves of paper torn
from military documents, English translations, coloring
books. Stories caught on the rigid glass. Knees in a gutter of
flies. I move my opened mouth hoping to produce screams,
this body has begun to shudder against the shards embedded in my skin. Sounds erupting from the hemorrhage. My
body vibrates with the setting storm.

I have become a sliver of the house, Grandpa tells me.

Out of a crooked doorway, a small girl lifts her head.
There is a ring of light in each eye that does not move to
the skin of her face. The reflection of circular bulbs made
for Grandpa's prying. Her sleeves are pulled up over her
knuckles and a small fingerless paw wraps around a corner
to prevent her body from displacing the air. Beside her,
against the wall, Grandpa's shadow looks like a mountain.
His head bobs up and down to focus his eyes on the bellies
of spiders and he bends their legs away from their torsos.
Their shells wanting to hug their bodies. In death. The girl
doesn't realize the shadow next to her is the body of her
grandfather. She thinks ghosts are chasing her.

Back into corners.

Speaking from the ground of meeting places, her girl-cous-
ins make up names for each other, write letters over the
concrete grid of their cities. They gathered folds of the earth
to hide one another. Neither one form nor another, but the
breath floating in-between the two. Grandpa uses language
to build myths into the creases of the land.

We are ourselves one body, kabuki masks of the diluted
clan. Facial features spread out like silt, crossed with white

mothers and white fathers until we are only connected by the thread of a vein, a name. The stories are pieced together over the pulse of blood and we are all versions of breast, bone and ligament.

Your lips are muscles of speech, Grandpa.
> They lock on your stories.
> They suffocate mine.

Grandma's cards sealed in all the shadows of the body. Her thin veined fingers twist flowers from their stems. She flattened the petals out between pages of memory and other people's words. Notebooks of dirt, rock and soil. Between the cross and the cross. They dried slowly. Smashed between worlds, their milk burst against the pages and their breath turned into ash. She tucked them into the folds of her mouth and turned them into God's words. Arranged the bodies of pressed flowers into the blank spaces for constructing cards. Pushed them around with her narrow filed nails that protrude from her skin until they had formed the face of God.

Her children became flowers pressed and flattened. Obeying the guidance of her fingertips, wounding the air with this thinning of stories.
Of souls.

When the flowers became the Noh Mask of God, she sealed them in with contact paper.

> Flowers that became
> the martyr of the body.

On Grandma's cards, Grandpa made a stage. He stood behind Grandma with his fingers locked together behind his
back. He dictated the life lessons for each occasion. Told her
to sign the cards with the three C's.
Christ.
Choice.
Consequence.

Signed the cards with love. Over the years, Grandma's
handwriting began to shake across the page. The letters
bleeding where too much pressure was put against the
paper with pen. Only Grandma's handwriting. In my mind
Grandpa's handwriting looked like the insects whose bodies
could not hold up under the strain of a pin prick, of his
entomological stage. Little silhouettes of bodies surrendering
death in language. I see their heads thrown back in song.

A rash of consequences when we deny our body the spirit of
our original bone.

I keep coming back to the cards. A Sunday late morning,
after donut holes and mouths full of Japanese names,
Grandma opens her organizer with small square com-
partments holding her dried flowers. The other slots hold
stickers, short strands of ribbon, stamps molded into our
family crest. She places her design on one side of the pastel
blue paper. Not solid blue, but scattered blue. White space
rising in the fibers of the card. The flowers flat and pressed,
soft like belly skin and warm like June air. They used to get
mixed up with the butterfly wings that sifted through the
air in Grandpa's study. Wings and arms and flowers. She
made beautiful cards with pressed faces. They were caught
in between the sticky side of the contact paper and the
porous blue paper. She would smooth out the pockets of air

from the middle towards the edges. Push the petals down into the fiber 'til the faces of the flowers were small designs masking the front of the card. Grandma's hands like rigid knots, holding the still life while her pen wrote stories on their wings.

TWELVE

Before primitive memories, these stones were old, ancient old, and cutting away at the sky. The temple's carved gray body, blackened and browned with earth and inclement weather. Gray haired, blue veined, breathing. Its edges rearing up like thick granite thread, lashing up into the blue. The bodies rubbing against rock.

Small orange robes weaved in and out of the hallways. Flicker of orange light. The deep tangerine peeked from the stone latticework, fluttered out of the fractured ruins. The men would not talk or look at me. They moved around my body like I was encased in glass. The dance pulled at my ribs. The breeze like breath underwater. I wanted to touch, to speak, to make the connection. But they could not talk to women.

I believed I diminished in their gaze past me. Disappeared, down the steps, my feet plummeting below the edges where stone meets air. The monks revolved above the ground. I, untethered in their gaze. Their waves of orange light, a baptism of sight. Their look, a language of gestures.

Give flight to the body. Without the body.

The temples at Angkor Wat in Cambodia were protruding bones in the land. The stone faces lifting out of the wind-worn walls, smiling from the belly of the earth. I pressed the pads of my fingers under my shirt, to the rim of my waist. I traced the profile of a smiling face and the rain started to fall.

In Laos the boys were not yet monks. Their hair is shaved away in patches I was told, a little at a time as they progressed through their monkhood. They blended into the rocks around them, gray and brown robes swung heavily around their tiny bodies. And they skipped and moved with sandals echoing across the gardened walkways. Their hair un-man-icured and wild as grass along the river. They held me in their eyes and did not know yet how to look away. Had not learned how to handle, to control their wonder. To learn to funnel desires into reason.

Three boys stood in a doorway. Their bodies tight together, cloaked in stone and oak. Their heads orbited around each others', restful in the light between them. Passing me a subtle message. But it was only their words in deep whisper to each other. I watched them from a doorway across the small yard. They looked up at me and smiled. One boy had a tooth missing, and the black of the hole made the other teeth glow against his brown face. I found home in the spaces in between them. To lift defining, rattle the myths at their root.

I practiced anonymity, between the pagoda's steps up to heaven and the deep curvature of the archways that linked me to the front gates. The prayers slipped around me and caught me in the palm of trailing breaths. I had not looked into a mirror in days. The sting of the cold ice against my lower front teeth moved in a chill down my body. Disap-peared into the stones. I imagined it carrying on, my body rooted deep into the layers of earth and stone. Toward the belly of the earth. The still water in the pool next to the pagoda magnified the light. Small bodies in the pool shim-mered, nickels spilling.

Without dreams or words I am nothing. Without my coun-try to inherit me, without the noise of unassuming stories, I

slip into the winter suit, the frightened fur, the animal that
came after the animal that I am.

Buoyed up on the backs of small foothills, the sun rises
towards the top of the tree line. The featureless dark rode
away on the skin of the Mekong and wrapped southward
into the distance.

New myths that un-know others.
The site of birth.

Begin again.

He is bringing blades, swinging blades, writing the line of light that floats heavy like a torrent of rain. He is subtle and dips between the *j* and *y* veining through the concrete footpath. He steps out on the ledge of his skin and tears my hair from the root. Keeps the blade in his mouth and seduces me with his eyes hanging dim over his bandanna. He doesn't blink and the night falls into his palm and he touches my skin at the belt loop. When he pulls I unravel into the tip of his knife. My bones fall loose into the soles of my shoes.

My knees leave inverted stones in the grass, he unbuckles my body from the ground and makes a house out of the A frame of my legs. There is grass in my teeth and plastic wrappers in my hair. He pulls at my hips and I rattle along behind his touch. A smear of white and black. The rip chord doesn't pull, holds back its release 'til I succumb to static and forgetting. Rip chord caught in the semen backing up in my body, the babies that aren't mine, lodged in my throat at the temper in his body. This contraption for remembering is rude and broken. It boasts it is brave, filing the edges of numbers down to the couth reserve of rapes and rupture.

I dream his dream. The snow covering the shoulder ripped through with arthritis. He pushes the scent of her into his lungs with thumbs and tongue and breath. He undoes his laces and removes his shoes. Piles them on the snow. The cold begins to numb his legs. His calves catching the ink white slipping from the sky.

In his dreams he holds her down and runs the rhythm of

his pulse from the back of her neck over the hills of her body. Her face canceled by pillow, her voice lost in whimper, waiting for minutes, waiting for release, waiting for the bruises to set in like little purple drops of amethyst on her hips. He doesn't feel her wriggling under his palms, doesn't feel the wave of her body lift and pull away from the ground. Doesn't feel the slim rope of her spine crack at the air. The lines of her ribs coat a great breath of pressure and bone. All he feels is himself extending inside her, feels the release of a days worth of silence that blisters at the seam of his sternum.

These
seams
hold
his
heat
steady
his
wrists
cracking
like
braided
straw

THIRTEEN

This is how girls speak with the boys in our family. Our touch is fragmented and we don't find the skin a comfortable place to meet each other. Even now as I hold my cousin's hand as she slips into her wedding shoes, she tenses at the knuckles. Our skin, three girl cousins, more like a landscape for hiding, behind water wells and tall birch trees. Hiding. To avoid the embarrassment of eyes meeting, we never let our breaths touch.

The phone rings.
Into the coiling lines wrapping over the earth I can hear their hearts beating. The cousins restless but still so quiet. They move their mouths to slip thoughts into electricity. Whispers that could not survive the fissure, if we were standing palm to palm.

I want to press my fingers against your mouth.
To feel my family breathe.

We speak in the dark to hide our bodies from knowing who each/other are. I think I can hear him, Grandpa sneaks in and rummages through our shadows and recreates figure-less lines. Stitching clothes back onto our bodies. Names. And he smells, like all of us.
Your grandchildren love and fear you.
Your children are still children playing in the drafts of a ghost.
I will burn in our hell, for every word that I write with my hands inside the body of the Father. The hell created from an absence of water. You speak to me in dreams. Sitting two generations away, a flame and body of broken skin. You are still the stones in my dreams.

Grandpa's eyes casting shadows on the stories of children. In fingers and tongues blackened. Dancing in ash, I form the ink for our fingerprints. Mouth prints.

I want to know you after all my lies and all my truths. I want to feed you my stories. Have them settle in the red language of your ribs. I want to enter the body of the father. You swivel your chair and place dead flies on the tongues of the family. Your body. Into the mouths of children.

FOURTEEN

Seducing you with stories of rape. I churn my legs pink,
bury them beneath a bandage of muscle and jean. Sun spent
skin. The way that women kneel, dropping the horizon to
the line of a man's belt. We take bread from the palms of
our fathers. Japanese woman and this mark. Those things
I love most confuse me. I resist the pokes and prods of the
other children. The fear of all the answers I didn't have,
waited at home for me. I pull my touch, my words, my voice
behind my eyes.

The wood door breaks into a square of light and the beau-
tiful boy tumbled out into the dark of 2 a.m., his wrists
wrapped in metal. I felt words forming at the rim of wounds.
He is gone. Steel mouths around his wrists, around his bone
deep freakish heat. The type without furniture and noise.
The heat is an open mouth.
And my wounds are open mouths.
And this body is speaking ahead of me.

Rising out of damp cotton. The same reverberating midnight. I create a point in my skin where night and day do
not touch. I have shattered the continuity into a body living
before voice. My voice recoils away from my body and I
wake up to pumping currents of screams and cries. There
are no dreams to tear me away from my flesh.

Trauma seeps out from under my nails. I am more than
scraping by. And past. This look across, sliding off his face.
In my dreams I meet him again and again and again and he
doesn't have a face. He is just the body of a boy.

I say this is where you disappeared. I am writing over you.

Across your joints I am playing with moments of infidelity.
Deception. Slivers in the autumn lawn. Turning desire to
dust and a stutter. I put my hand to the sun. Divide the
slices of light to devour your movement. This you is no
longer just you, Grandpa. It is the undoing that singed our
first words.
I am.
Gone.

Reaching out to swallow. Inhuman.
The mouth so wide as if to split suddenly at the corners.
Fear is a flood. The dam stopped up for so long.

Rivers of blood that carry memory. Fear as fond as touch
and resilient and present and speaking. The dialogue of fear
and the body is a heated mess. His tongue flicking the top
of his mouth. I imagine he had no tongue. No language.
Instead he invaded the room with the fierce body of a child
before words.

Stuck like a sliver in the body vein. He had my heart in his
hands. I would prod at his scarred body to step back off of
my tongue.
The blade. Image to eye to memory.
Boys will be boys.
Girls must act as if boys will always just be boys.

I imagine the way my hands would smudge dirt into the
tears I wiped from his face when he tried to cry out for his
mommy. The beautiful boy. I wouldn't do it with whiskey
on my breath. Something clean. Something wet on the
rocks. Something that would sting his eyes when I breathed
heavy and hard on the back of his neck. I would use more
words. No elevated grunts. There will be no kissing on that

night. No. Just the last great move as I tear the belt straps away from his pants as he holds tight to the faded jean gaping around his waist. I'd whisper that the music is supposed to soothe him.

Drown out
someone else's screams.

I tear my skin away from my body. Rape dying to be raped again. For some sort of reversal.
You don't want me saying these things.
You would rather hear me scream.
I would rather hear a scream.

The beautiful boy. His pen deep and writing on the inside of my legs. When he bent over to drop me towards our ground, the ink began to spill out all over everything. The scratching. A small child not able to turn over by herself. But I deserve all of this. Could not have it any other way.

When I close my eyes, this violence becomes language. The tightness in my palms draws blood and I am a beautiful boy resting a hand on the back of Vodka girls. Reclaiming what is left of un-ravaged skin. She gathered from the debris what all women gather. The panties. A few threads always hanging around the waist band. Then she went for what all men go for. And quick. The bra. The wire had been loose for a while, protruding through a whole at the armpit, now it hung out. Sharp. Made for tearing and punching through.

I am just weeding away at the soft spot. My desire. When men touch me, I imagine women's lips and whispers. In dreams, I rape myself in order to shed the shame. Women that rape themselves. Acts of violence and the release, like a peace that follows. The cold moment before dawn. Cooling in pools drenching the in-between of our legs. I cannot be honest enough to let myself love someone else. I am at odds with my body. With what it says to me when the heat is contained. I am the wound between my legs.

It's the battering of the body. Turning it into something that has forgotten how to speak. When I reached up from a place of no words, my body began to speak its living to my mother. This turn in the room of hands. My own blood beating. Against the paper, porous skin, failing tongues of women bleeding to cover up the naked space.

In the action of splitting, I pull the teeth from my name and hollow out a hole for uttering. Just at the edge of speaking I become a woman of sounds. To half annunciate, covered in breath, I have beaten my body to a place of ravaged language. In pulling the rape from the muscle, I replace it with my own savage impalement of the skin.

Rape drops from my body like the strings of a ventriloquist. I am attached to it, even while it dances another story. We are two mouths moving.

I deserve what I deserve what I want.

FIFTEEN

I am haunted before the words that tremble, wretch. I am
haunted by the places that can't be reconciled. I move on
the surface of brittle land, leather land, textured green. The
Killing Fields, fragile and entwined with swaths of bone.

Places named according to their purpose. The story that
they leave to the voices from nearby school children. Life
so close to death. Words that speak with immediacy, the
Killing Fields, as if still in movement, carrying out genocide.
Bodies not yet done dying, an artery in a dream that rup-
tures but is contained. The fields still killing. No, that is
wrong,
Begin again.

I read books lost in silver trinket corners. Feel the stories
galvanize. These stories bound in myth. Shoulder to shoulder in conversations over people who could not understand
that killing does not conclude. Even after, the dead cannot
be counted. Stories that lay quiet even less, than the shape
of a ruin.

The walkways wrap around dips in the earth. They are lit a
deep green, opening the flatness of the earth into rippling
emerald waves. Trees spot the land and hold too tightly to
death in their trunks. The rigid booms of their arms like
mothers, pleading with the sky for baby's blood to be pulled
from the layered bark. Layered over blood, over death,
tripping the wires of the sun and refracting light from their
bodies of rings. This place where men become babies and
babies die before they are men.

I whipped my head back against the sky, snapped my eyes

away from the ground. A wing to shield the loss. Lost plummeting baby bird, toward the bones in Cambodia. In the ground I could hear the children crying. A brook of rippled language running their trails into cries and then silence. The little knuckle children screamed for mama before they were swung sideways against trees. The men recoiled into their mother's womb as the Cambodian boys tucked there noses behind their peaceful scarves, checkered stones in white water, and put the point of a spade against the back of necks.

The stones yawn gray in the ground. The grass swallows them. Between the shards of light that break through the tree's veined branches I remember the twilight that grandpa last saw. Before his body broke into streams, into DNA twisting towards the end of his language. Wrapping their tails around grandpa's throat. One last breath.

Good bye, Grandma, his skin whispers.
She closes her eyes and wishes for new Bible pages found under earthen bowls providing hints between the living and the dead. I hoped to find the restless words we haven't found yet, Grandpa, dancing between the earth and bones, pressed against each other like hands in prayer.

Grandma presses her fingers into his mouth and prays for her own death. Keep the door open. And she holds her breath and waits for Grandpa to seize her by her apron. But he runs away, now that his legs are working and the strings are cut from around his looping fingers. His rest comes. And Grandma sits alone. The light caught in the dust throws a little life into the room. Under her dyed black hair now thin like feathers, she closes her lips to dry. A solid crest of dirt and legend.

From behind me I heard PK whisper *they most commonly called for their mothers before the blow was given.* PK, our guide through Cambodia, still looking for his brothers and sisters. Hoping they found a cave to hide in. I would give them a feather. Wash them in the wind.

The belly of the earth swells. Dives down toward small bone fingertips. The knuckles still bleeding in sister's dreams. The sky full of light, a tower erected to raise the bones away from the stories cluttered in bowls in the ground. But the ancestors of the dead don't lay flowers here. Their dreams are to burn the bones, send them home. The flesh of our fathers released to the open air, I hear their cries towering above the whispers in the ground. I sit against the tire of the chicken bus, my skin layered brown in the humidity, heat, and earth.
Watch the bodies in the ground rearrange.

Rearranged in the ground. Under the tunnels of water feed-ing roots, the small orifices in the human dirt feeding grass, the bones rearrange themselves into new bodies that live in the earth. The fibula dances into the mouth of a mother who used to cry for her daughter to stop all this screaming. *Wipe your face, j. Lean into me. Lean into me.* And I see my grand-mother holding Grandpa as his body contracts into dips and sealed off pockets of air. The ground holding its breath.

The waist of the trees taper in then bow broad, back into the bank of bodies and small streams. Small skulls scattered and stratified. A mouth wide and open. The jaws stuffed with pebbles and dried blood. Now sucking on the fibula. Back to birth. Back to the body of a child. Pacified.

The way that a doctor rearranges bones, rearranges the joints like a puzzle, to make them fit. Grandpa with his tweezers. Floating between the dead insects and his eyes. *Blink-less, practice makes perfect.* Bending the legs in or away from the body, straitening torsos and then harnessing them with a pin-prick. His entomology, a map for our wings. Metal rigging bodies meant for movement, meant to make their own sounds. And the dead insects open up as their bodies deteriorate. Against Grandpa's will, they are in a box cut off from voice and air. But still their bodies change. Even in death. He taps his fingers against the trail that their skeletons leave across his collapsible table. And his breath stirs them. His exhale unexpected. His chair leaning in towards the dead.

Interlude

I resigned to be a body in the ground. To untouch. Begin to fear all the things I tucked inside my sheets at night. Tucked between the feathers collapsed against my body, inherent in dreams.

The part that I am afraid,

is really me.

To fix your face now beautiful boy to the inside of my thigh.
You fucked pleasure out of me. Now, rape is the only thing
with enough fire to cauterize the vein.

Sand down the lacuna I shield along bone.

Run your patched calloused palms and rickety knuckles
down 'til the hair breaks off into air. Walk away. Tie your
drawstring tighter. Don't let this touch in, as it fixes to move
under gray cotton. In. Through the side of your underwear.

This air.

That has become the suture in my breath.

Grandpa moving in the shadows of a room.

Circa 1943. A boy in a box, in a cage, in a country.

Further into the hallway I saw nothing but sterile white light. The fixtures of a family I would not tell about these things. Because their ghosts were frowning.

We were ghosts before we were people. The echo of high-lighted Bible pages creased and creased again. There are no forgiving words. I will eat every last one of them. Swallow the chorus. Spit and sweat.

You are not here with me.
On top of the industrial sheets.
Out of my body.

We have judged the past of words.

I say he is beautiful because he looked so good in black.
Shoulders round over cuts of muscle, gripping handle bars.
Hips. When he wrapped his hands around the body of his
glass stem, the wine coursed like blood in his starched
calloused hands. The beautiful boy rearranged the necks of
Beam and Walker to fit the movement of his arms.

Lifted things meant for two boys to lift. Sweat beading
around the openings of his clothes.

The beautiful boy. Don't name him.

His density opens me. At the seams I am still at appeal.
Growing there, where the bone thickens and hinges into
the snow-white light. Baked beige, blood red fingertips. It is
my own prying inside of me. And I am bound to them still,
after all this time.

He was immediacy and you. I.

My hands were under the pillows when the beautiful boy
ran his fingers over the slit of my mouth.

Must have been drooling, dreaming. Vodka induced sleep.
Arms don't move when they are lodged under pillows.
Twisted out of my pants. Meant to twist away. That pair
had never let me down. Sat above the soft flesh of my back.
Along the lines of my small protruding abdomen. In summer they dampened around the seat. Dried before the spots
became visible. The beautiful boy pulled at stretching fabric.
Wrapped hands around flimsy belt loops and pushed my rib
cage into the musk mattress. Or was it the grass wet with
the recent rain. Mist on the scars of remembering. Reduced
into a pile of sweat and jeans bunched around my knees.

If I am losing my mind then the hands touching flesh
between my legs are his. Mine a bit more slender. The nails
longer and squared at the edges.

And if I am losing my mind then my hands are pushing
against flesh towards his calloused misused hands.

And my hands cannot reach.
My skin gets in the way.
The soft flesh covering my belly has begun to mold to the synthetic fibers in his blanket and I am trapped. Against my own flesh.

Psalms in the dirt.

I am still inside this always, remembering.

If I am losing my mind.

And I still can't speak towards the story's end.
There is no
anymore.

I track the dictionary each night in my dreams. The language
is in images I once knew. Forgotten language. Never learned
in measurements and letters. The cold black center, lid
coaxed to close. Just right.

                    The look. A conversation between eyes.

I have forgotten the language that washes in before words.
Around the ankle. Spoken into skin with caresses. Eyes on
the stage.

The room is empty.

SIXTEEN

The photograph becomes the severed door of the story,
to close off and open rooms. I am back in the drought of
shadows. Light that illuminates. I stand a foot away from
the baking image of my brother, unable to reach through
the black phone at the end of a metal coil, I place it in his
hands as I turn away. Turn toward. The between of fathers.
The one that is my brother. The one that is my father. The
bodies of men. Grandpa moving his fists and flexing fingers
to pluck at the tendons. His heat warps their bodies into
hollowlanguage. Our song.

His eyes worked by searching. Frown lines deepened and he
built a tomb of answers. Moving between black and white.
The shades of gray made my father's eyes wander away
from the threads binding him to the body of the family.
Gray didn't explain death. When my voice broke on a dirt
mound, he began to imagine all the things that would begin
to build my house of stone. Out of the polished roots of our
home, in the rubble of his wishes, he puts his hand over my
face to disguise the fact that I was a girl. The girl parts of
me deepened into shades of ash.

The dark midnight of boys being boys. It does not disappear.
It only shifts.
Into bone.

Grandpa is creating electricity in order to be closer to God.
As he moves, the room heats and a pulse widens to the
window panes. Rubbing its blood-filled veins over the thin-
framed glass. The pulse of the father is the sound of electricity moving up and down the scent of skin.

He used to tell us little girls made better doors than windows. We would be standing against the wall. Grandpa moved through rooms without force or voice. He circled the house, doors always open, each photograph, book, petal in its place. Our small hands tucked behind our backs, against walls.

You are the blooming vision of Grandma's roses. When you pricked your palms the blood dried into scars that began to trace the first words.

Grandpa bought a house to throw stones against his sorrow. When his family was interned during World War II, they lost everything. The rhythm of his need rattled the wind. His desire splintered the body of the house and his children scattered into the arms of American men and women. Trapped in a space of scars and wet earth. Resonating out of pores and heat.

Grandpa sold his piano for five dollars to the men driving a truck to haul away misfit Japanese possessions. The keys were met by foreign fingertips. Songs laid to rest so that other compositions could be collected in the air at Tule Lake. Grandma's fingerprints were buffed away. Then Grandpa joined the army. He told the story with a stiffened back and an upturned mouth. The photographs translate his pride, one foot kicked over the other, a cocked head, a smirk. His uniform beautiful on his young body. Grandma's face upturned towards the light. Searching for God.

Grandpa translated his native tongue. The language of his people. As they hung like painted figurines on posters and in the static of TV screens. Grandpa spoke the languages of two countries that bore away into a thousand lines of blood and soot.

I smell the scent of your country. A thin skin of water
running over rocks at midnight. The smell of railroad ties
behind Grandpa's house. The smell of alcohol drawing
oil out of the skin. Your troubled land stealing all of your
stones. You balanced your body between earth and heaven.
Walking away made the ash flake from your feet. Calloused
soles striking the air. Your movement is wind whipping the
pages of this Bible. White-washed skin covered utterances of
foreign tongue.
He filed his children between the pages of his Bible.
Rubbed their names against dusted fables.
                    I became your Eve, Grandpa.

Men have become earth under my tongue. Gold flakes on
the back of summer sand. My mouth stretched around the
wilting Birch pulled towards the hardened ground, where
your river could not reach.

Release memories to reason. Viscous tears fall into lines to
grease the suture, undo the scab from healing.

Onto pages.

Naming sounds that come around the corner of the white
stained hallway. Grandpa's dust-filled mouth cracked the
air with severed sentences. English embedded with Japanese spears. I tell my skin stories of what stories you might
be telling, Grandpa. The frayed rope binding your house of
words. You gnaw at the fiber covered in Japanese figures.
Girls pushed back to the edge of symbol. Grandma says her
grandma had black teeth stained to show her samurai line.

My scars mock you. Closer to speaking. Whispers that close
in on the front end of a trailing word. Falling short of

finding. In the dive and scrape of our nails against the page, Grandpa, your prayers have gone to recess. I am your Eve, Grandpa.

I am your escape.

From your country.

When they moved into their new house on a well respected
cul-de-sac backed up to the agitated belly of the levee, their
lives began to build the seams of a new narrative. A mile of
concrete separated the new house from the tracks that ran
through the backyard of the old house. The old house was
the beginning of memory. And of forgetting.

The boxcar-shed housed a thousand insects floating like an-
gels in alcohol and the ricochets of bouncing light. The old
house, the one story holding a thousand stories of summer
heat, single sprinkler habitats, radio flyers and foil hanging from baking trees to keep the bugs away. But the birds
came to taunt the shiny treasures and we cloaked ourselves
in the arms of fruit to find blossoms of shade. The birds
would peck at the air. Twitching their necks, trying to shake
loose the heat.

Then the new house. All these new vacant walls that were
filled with light. Shadows maneuvered through fields of
dust. Grandpa unpacking the new beginnings of old junk
as he rounded into his seventies. Old man ties and t-shirts
covered in ladybug graphics. They unpacked no old furniture into the rooms filled with mahogany silk window
dressings. Community spaces for the visiting. They sat on
designer couches and filtered the old things into smaller
rooms and corners. Doors that locked from the outside. The
monju cakes became few and hidden. Pushed to the sides of
Grandma's kitchen cabinet housing her hand painted cups.
The cakes squatting next to Grandma's ocha, the tea jars
encircled in broken leaves. The trip back to Japan never
happened for the grandchildren. Instead we explored Dis-
neyland and yearly trips to Mexico. The desire so deep and

shattering within Grandpa that we must always be American.

We must always remember that we are not American.

But he stood on the back patio in the evenings, looking
through the blue hours toward the edge of the yard. He
could make out the red fence and back gate of the old
house. He stood there like he was waiting for that red door
to open, for his children to come tumbling through.

Grandpa became an entomologist working with tiny bodies
he could name and prick and control. His winged family.
His family dancing with their skirt of legs. We were not
allowed in the lab he kept at home. Our little cousin games
taking us too near his work. We wanted to use the micro-
scope to see into the lines on our palms.

It's through the shoulder blades that the pin slides through
the body. The pin that writes the bad blood across the single
stab against the board. The mind impaled with the sounds
of scraping boxes. Their hinges creak when Grandpa seals
them. The glass window for a top. The bodies of insects on
display for Christmas presents, warnings. Pine that smells
of mothballs. Tiny tombs saturated with the scent of chemi-
cal stains and typewriter ink.

Through the lens of my grandfather I find that the flesh is
pieced together by words. I look hard and long at the skin
bandaged by sun and threaded cloth. Small scales of deep
naming and the blank space of the utterings of the daughter. Thin white tags. Polysyllabic titles. Gravestones.

Pieced between skin wars and race wars. The battles are
told without me. Trapped between the borders of skin and

biology the words begin to disintegrate like the bodies of the beautiful blue moths spreading like water into their resting places. Fighting for a spark that will ignite memory. Set fire to all the bridges. Bone layers that twitch and vibrate. Heat driven by our histories that expand into the shape of the atom bomb.

I want to peel away your reason, Grandpa.

Find what mythologies lay there.

I remember the still night when I drank myself into a bedtime story. The dream released in the form of laughter as the worlds of my dreams came closer to the tip of my tongue. I never laugh so hard as I do in dreams. Wet laughter, tears, and joy. My body writes itself in dreams. Sleep is only a lighting change. A movement in time. Always my present.

Sleep is not an escape.

But a descent.

I am my brother and my cousins. I speak the stories that
I have created to take the place of the ones I cannot write.
I open the mouth of the Father and find we all sit legs
crossed on their devouring tongues. We became a part of
another people's history. The girls hold our wombs tightly
when we sleep. We feel the language of the family is saturated in the bodies of girls. We try our hardest to keep our
legs open without letting all the words fall out.

We have the stories that have been told to us, Grandpa.
We have the stories that we felt under the weight of your
hands.
They have become embedded in skin.
As they formed our bodies, we came into conflict with the
stories that we were making.
I go back to pace the hallway of the house we have built,
Grandpa. Everything has changed. That's too easy. The
house has changed its clothes. Its body memory still utter-
ing, with a trampled voice.
Our Bible is mute.

I want hands like a weaver. Take a thread through the center of Hiroshima. The movement follows the explosion into
the skin. The shadow left on the wall by the incinerating
body. The flash of light moves outwards and bellows into
the circles of a rounded back. The light triggers the needles,
ready to rip through the mother and into the child. Severed
from the earth, from the Father, the body should not have
had a pulse. Your stories mark the entrance wound, Grandpa, through the binding of the Bible. My stories have begun
to open old seams.
To begin again.

I have the anxious overload of a body too aware of itself.
Over the years my cousin and I wrote about love and death
and fear to each other. We drift in and out of a shoebox of
folded paper. Always loving and stitching webs. In the tra-
peze of their time, fear has turned sacred,
        my paralysis.
Chasing one another, we fall into each other's arms. To not
be touched.

The body is like a promise. The ear withstanding the heat
of battering palms, a promise. I don't want the parallel
scratches on the white patches of my arms to say anger or
victim or voiceless. I need a story about undoing. I need to
walk my body back through the crumbling storyline so I
don't assume my own victim. I need to undo my shaping.
Breathe with the tempo of the language my body is wandering with, within memory. The way we walked as children.

I have mirrored the moving of men's tongues. The way
they puncture the room, spark the air. Lash like coat tails.
Harbor their swollen wet words under the skin of my
clothes.

I have not been a woman for so long.

YONSEI

Dear Grandpa,

Is that you, dragging your feet again. The needle I fixed
through my own torso, from front to back, is slowly losing
its temper. I am polarized, pulled at the joints and spinning
around the stem of your desire. Silence in a quartered box.

They cry tears for you and buff your infamous dead. The
insects revolving on an axis of gray, your steep pins that
prick and pierce like incisors, like those men sweating their
names on my back.

I want to be your blossom, Grandpa.

You told me that naming is sacred. Your typewriter clicks,
small high heel steps on tile, anchor my name in word.

I am the shrapnel of the family.

Your death,
Your granddaughter

LITTLE BIRD

Cancer crept through his catacombs, his skeleton worn
ragged like country gravel. Eyes like saffron. The memories
fade, I can count on this, but have left their signatures.
They leave rumors under pillows. Like the cooler pockets of
tucked night. I watched his body slack, wanted to be interior
to his dying.

I tell myself rumors that he is not dead. There are dimples
in the land where his body should be, they are tinted sepia
and spreading like ink, to places under my feet. The ground
respires, is pocked across countries, and he is restless, even
in death.

The stories I tell myself are faulty at best. Every inch of the
road I've created in this story, has marks of memories that
everyone tells me are not true. I can't remember the rain.
Just the warm, beige sheets on his bed. The red alarm clock
squatting in the light. The porcelain head of a dog that held
his glasses away from the dust.

Every part of me sees his death in my own way. The days
were always sunny. He had radiation treatments. He was
always dressed in white near the end. Grandpa could not
recognize me without context. The only time I ever saw him
cry, in my life, was the last time I was with him. I should
have taken the sheets that hid his sagging body. I should
have clipped the feathers that hung in his eyes.
I should have tasted every tear,
that they say he never cried.

I am slipping inside your Noh mask, Grandpa.
I am the pariah to your breath.

SEVENTEEN

His gun rattled in his fingertips. Teeth hammered against
one another like rows of ivory beads lifting and falling.
He said nothing with his lips parted, but his eyes looked
far past the scattered Beer Chang bottles on the table and
I wonder who pressed his uniform each day. Who takes
a moist cloth to the cuffs of his pants and wipes away the
afternoon dust. Who checks his gun to make sure it is un-
loaded.

He is a canyon. A deep cave in Laos where, pressed back
against the tight veins of its rock, lie small statues of Bud-
dha and trinkets of lost ones. He is a lost one. His stories
are somewhere behind the far away look in his eyes. They
blister to be heard.

The man was re-educated away from his home, separated
from his memories. I want to press my mouth against the
palm of his shaking hand.
Listen to what stories lie there.

He looked into me, past the body. My skin unfolded, flesh
like flowing tears. When I close my eyes and look away
I feel him there still, rocking softly as to not disturb too
much air. He was close to the edge of my chair. The unfin-
ished wood soaking up the sweat of its occupants. I opened
my eyes and he was there standing over me. His body and
his stories detached into air. Taught me leave, in the sorrow
of skin.

His body in a crescent of light. Fingers fluent in channeling
air. The ripe and worn beds of grass raising him away from
the earth. His sentences are athletic, I see the curvature of

his language released from his mouth as he whispers wind words. The land forming sentences in his body.

In ripples
and currents
and stones.

I left him with my mouth full of rice. A baptism. In the joints that hold my body together I place small alms for the children. If there are children. They whisper to me that pain keeps you conscious.

I leave this place, Grandpa.
Leave my life in a single fingerprint on the torso of a teak tree.

I dream of the rape, the rape that will cleanse. The rape
beautiful enough to wash clean the soot, the stagnant water,
the body's apocalypse.

I dream rape in the way that I used to dream flying. The
freeing, the tall grass prairie opening up for miles and
miles, but alone I felt always. This always and this dream
that housed a flying child. The grass growing tall over people's heads, the stalks splitting their images in two. I fragment like hot glass in cold water. The burn breaks through
and down into the language that I have thought forever
I would know. On my tongue there is a splinter, it pivots
toward blood.

Fingerprints and child and rupture. To reconcile. I dream
of the rape that is good, that will allow me back my dreams.
The substance of night that does not create a ring around
your eyes without dusk. In the dream I am a boy, always.
Pushing a girl into the earth beside the rust of abandoned
train tracks. Her body billows in the heat. The cloud that
erupts from the dust swallows our nearness and I feel what
it might have been like to be inside of myself. To grip the
wing, the blade, the dark tattoos of my back.

Baby bird.

The chirp now a stutter, I slide the body inside me, press
face to pillow until the words themselves cry out. The sound
of the body saving itself. My fists tight with envy become
our jeans tight with envy. To prepare a meal ripe for all
these abrasions, to induce violence that cleanses one last
time.

When I write, I leak ink by the heat of my body. The pressure and burn of wounds rot with want. The need for the space to either disappear or transform. The skin that folds between my legs, my lips, my eyes, my hands. This netting, is again, a fingerprint.

EIGHTEEN

The slow boat through Laos had just our small group of travelers on board, an American and a handful of Australians. I opened the list of names in my palm just enough to see my grandfather's leaded strokes. I closed the list along the worn crease. The water in the Mekong was like rust pumping through the vein of a jungle. The banks spotted with thatch and teak homes. The green raised along the sides, dense and vibrant. Arms that were raised, clothed, to the horizon. Up towards the sun. And the body bobbed, face down, caught on a limb that was caught below the surface. Slumped shoulders and a bowed head, breathing water.

My back was to the oncoming current. I sat facing the past 'til it was memory.

The leaves spinning in the vein of rust.

We kept moving forward, my back entering onward. Bouncing the scent of dragon fruit and wet rock against my spine. Watching each new scene replace the old one.

There are no words that make sense inside the rust of drifting.

A life in reverse, opening backwards. My face missing what it means to face. My breath spinning in my stomach and the loudness of the motor, not loud enough.

The body lying face down with the ears bobbing like baby ducks in the water. I imagined that the bodies lying with their faces in the wet earth of the Mekong, slip their souls into the silt on the river floor. Tickled by the current they seep under the layers of plant and bone and earth. Eyes searching and then slipping out of their sockets. This movement of coming and going.

The wind picked up and the water rippled behind the boat, in front of me. Time passing us, Grandpa. It wrapped around the curve of the earth.

The red river no longer broken by the blue whispering mass.

NINETEEN

I am un-memorizing myself. After so many years, as the
body replenishes itself, sheds its layers, fades into a cascading dream. The memories catch light on the leaves, in the
crippling shadows and quiet, they move down my belly,
down my legs, to the ground. The muscles always pressing
against the light.

My mother called me to speak of your death. To tell me you
were dead. Pacing outside the fence above sunset cliffs, the
small insects tap across my skin. The small mosquito bloated with my stories, spread red across my flesh. The movement back. Stories moving around the stone in my gut.

Your stories are fingertips voice thumbprint on the slope of
my swinging ribs.

When Grandpa let the tears write scripture on his face, I
imagined I could see my own fault lines. The same wrinkle
along the right side of our mouths. The same fissure between our brows.

The shards of the mirror are the task of paper. Pen. Speak
onto the skin, onto the site where I hope to meet you one
day, Grandpa. Watching the craved understanding of the
suit-less skeleton reveal itself. Drawing on the mirror I am
tracing over my own reflection. I find the ash of his body
saturates the water.

Grandpa was a hammer. The gentle tapping of his scripted
beliefs chiseling silence into air. Found its rage on pieces of
skin. They centered on the war and wounds.

I stood in my Grandfather's doorway. Hands curling around the metal hinges waiting for the air to move. From a swivel chair, my grandfather mimicked the dead insects floating in alcohol. As he sucked in the fumes of decaying bodies, he turned towards the open door. Flipped the rims of his glasses towards the ceiling. When he saw me, he said nothing, twisted back towards the dead. The gaping jaw of the swinging door created brutal squeaks when children walked in hallways.

Memory burns pain into the cross hairs of the curtains. At hours relied on for light, he synthesizes my desires into a peach boy dreaming. At the foot of the rust colored carpet are the mouths of the men. Their tongues whip the air. Spit dust and fire. The little girl growing out of a wall wound.

In the back of the bedroom near the ironing board and doorless closet, the child is packed away in cardboard skin. As I am un-memorizing my ways of forgetting, I go back to the photos of home before I realized that home was a dream. I hold my brother in the breath of my reach. His small shiny head fitting in the folds of my neck. I will hold him close to me for the rest of his life, while he dies a thousand deaths that his boy.man.japanese skin cannot handle. We pray to prevent the Psalms of the soul from reaching past our generation.

Our bodies un-shape vertical language. Grandpa began to flatten into the space of his foreign land.

Grandpa was a stone split by freezing water. His ribs twisted into the body of a child conceived before blood. He reared back into the brick solace he denied his bones, locked himself in glass panes and angles of hardwood and photographs.

You are a ghost, Grandpa.

Begin again.

The rupture formed the trail of his mouth.

It twisted with the sounds of dying. Broke the hinge of the family. Splintered the skin of his children. Between the mountains and the sea, the city became a graveyard. We began to build over the fracture that had the absence of thirst. Began to darken with ash. Wrapped ourselves in wood wrapped in concrete.

Moving through the forest, the trees and stones surrounding my feet began to vibrate. The collapsing spring of my mouth moved to shake skin loose from muscle folding away from bone. The cleansing letters of mud writing, pushes the coarse earth into the protrusion of rock shoulders and spinal stone steps. The knobs of knees and fists and granite legs open to the flesh valleys falling between them where I want to lay my hands. Find a mother somewhere who loves my father. Convince me. Begin again.

In borrowed March, I look for my father's old shirts that carry the scent of heavy oak. The beautiful racket that could erupt from him when he first met my mother.

His body overlooked the parade of words that were demolishing him even then. Then you put stones in the family pockets and tried to walk on water. As if a gift.

I am your newest iteration. I am a sketch of your history. We are each others' clothes. Textural refuge. When I dream I bury us here. Our ever other.

My mother's double negative cracked under the summer harvest. Her hands ripping through the canvas. Overturned shell. Evening prayers. Her heart mended to the dress. Her body carnival. She fought against the desire to reduce her myth into feed. The reel. Bend the scent of the storm. My mother disarmed beneath the trees in the country. Let fall her bones of birch to clatter around me. Her breath caught in the pause. The sundown like his torture over the northern constellations. Mother moving to shield against my father. Again, a trick of light. This is how we begin.

I wish for her green language of alfalfa, wet rotting fences propped up in the field, small birds shaking away the wet. Want to feel them spill names all over the ground, soak like milk toward our stories.

The scorched sky is the flint ravaging bone in the shadow. Night sets in, between buried letters, notes, conversations. Changes the color of skin to a squint of lines drawn into dust. Lines that move like Grandpa's scripted characters, running up and down the earth. They turned into the first slivers of language falling from the tall birch trees in Grandpa's ravine. High rocks that began to blush into violet red light. Bruised the ground into flesh.

Language disappears. Took my body with it. In the folds of peach and yellow, my skin is thirsty, for want of water. I run my skin brown under the Tabasco sun. At the end of the day I shape shift into bone.
In order to remember.

Grandpa pinned flies to cardboard canvases. Sturdy board that was designed with small flaking deaths.
Wings of butterflies.

Spiders.
Children.

He fluttered the dense cushions across the only couch in
the photograph room, smelled like rubbing alcohol, hidden
monju, and sugar burning in the sun. I pressed my face
into the center, dipping in with the small secure pinch of
a button. Smelled Grandpa two rooms away beneath the
magnifying lamps. Could taste the small vials leaking fumes
into the room. Sweet bean cakes warming under Grandma's
fingertips and Grandpa's flies, legs floating in the currents
of breath in his office, sitting in the wet corners of his eyes.

His trust that his fingers would do what he told them, keep
the small bodies of insects together as he attaches them to
the spindle of example. Typed their names on small strips of
notecard paper. Delivered unto them the voices that sounded like letters colliding, turning them into bodies without
souls.

The journey from the loose walls that held the bulging
sounds of a family displaced and locked into the tight skin
of bombs. Throbbing bundles of his stories that began long
after he was born a boy. He was never a child who spoke
unforgivable words. He has been a man tangled in these
threads for all of his life.

I have forgotten where we started. And Grandpa you sat,
uttering the old words. Wanting them to make sense in a
different world. *I am a fixture of your desire. For naming.* Only
language in sounds, already forgetting, under the beating
wings of dying flies, the body.

TWENTY

The search is to find my body under the ripped ground of a country I have never known. Tie bodies back to the land and remove muted screams from the violent whisper. Girls are a shadow left against the wall after the hydrogen bomb.
My family.
My stories.
To find this anonymity and start again.

We staggered chairs in the grass. The family. Wrapped in the wood, fence, brick, and drowning leaves of the squatting oak, the family moved to house Grandpa in the edges of our bodies. His eyes moved in and out of focus. Glazing over for minutes of blank conversation, heaving without the blink that would break up the large gusts of wind shuffling us into awkward angles. Waking orbs of brown that would move across my face. Stringing us together in a series of stares that familiar years had given us. His eyes still begging questions. Even in the twilight, his eyes failing him, his body failing him, his mouth drying in the air.

He would not ask for help to wipe the leaves off his shirt. Their dried edges snagging the loose folds of his polo. Holding those photographs in my hands, I try to find the look lying there that suggests he sees the camera. Knows it is there to hold him forever. In a negative. In a frame. His glance that would steepen for seconds. That stare I hoped he could shake for a moment, blink back the person that faded more than memories.

Where did he go. His wings that crippled beneath our touch as cancer devoured his body.

The day before, he would be walking around the family room in his underwear. The white aged into beige. As close to naked as he would allow in order to be closer to the air. As close to being present as he could stomach.

When Grandpa could, he tried to untwist from the bed, his body bound upright, wriggled free from the sheet and left its empty husk. Propped his body up against the headboard. Charted his way through the Metro. Down through the weather and obituaries. Last reminisces of Japanese names turning into newsprint and recycled paper.

His curves bulging beneath the electric blanket. The wire running along his hips cold and worn down. Feet crossed. Knees kissing away any intrusion of air. His breath inhaling names from the creases of the newspaper. Speaking names he hadn't spoken in 60 years.
Grandma would take in the names between nods as she pulled flowers from their stems, placed them in between pages of
dictionaries,
Bibles,
thick catalogs of insects and children's stories.
Stack their words onto Grandpa's tongue.

He pulled their memories from the back of his hair, rubbed them against the softening grain of his skin. Rolled them between his fingers.

He worked in riddle language. Bouncing back and forth between the finite alphabet and the bending bodies of symbols that held breath and light. Limbs of twisting painted bodies. His eyes must have grown tired after they folded countries against each other. He pressed his thumbs against the fading stories. Life compiled in columns, measurements. His body like his work. Like his insects. Denied fresh air, hovering in death above the foundations of their last resting places. Preserved bodies in mid-movement. Crooked, arched, and still.

He touched what was left of his underwear band, pulled it to press against the drooping mouth of his navel. He crushed the paper in his hands. Inched his legs over the edge of the bed into the square of light crossed in shadow. The vacuum cleaner creating lines that stretched the body of the house, all threads leaning the same way. East towards their rising sun, moving its final frequencies to turn Grandpa's sky into a burning red. Grandma smoothed the blankets behind Grandpa as he pulled his body along the side of the bed. Grandma's hands on his back. The touch without speaking, in palms and fingertips. Stale air and the sky against his chest, a centipede stale on his skin, directing the eyes of his children south.

He wrote in the bindings of Bibles. His body wrenching Japanese from his skin to surround the English in crowded bodies. Silver-lined pages tissue thin. Rubbing Japanese symbols we could not read into the sounds of our own shadowlanguage. Will them into accepting each other. His mouth full of jumbled time, reined in by the coarse hide of the family tongue.

He whispered into the lapel of his robe about missing years. The sounds of his voice too vulnerable for children to hear. It sounded like rocks returning to the bottom of a river. In pieces. Baseball games behind chain link fences, the leather spheres torn on barbed wire and Grandma's form shifting behind the heavy sheets. Make believe walls for Japanese internees.

Grandpa pressed his hands into his receding abdomen. Hunching over the slice of air entering through the slit of his mouth, his teeth dried to show the threads of worn enamel where the threat of too many stories had worn away and gnawed at his body. In the loose fold of his skin where the muscle and bone had begun to back away, Grandpa invented scripture that would make going towards death easier. He prepped his body in moments of consciousness for the time when he might let go. The scripture sank into his veins, sent words through his body. Writing skin secrets.

Take this body child.
Forget your stories
You are a ghost.

The tape holding photographs to the edges of cupboards, backs of doors, the rim of lamp light, began to loosen their grip. The photographs began to fall away from the house. Back of the burdened skeleton shedding names, faces, measurements of bodies twisting in time with the camera's deflection, eyes that wouldn't meet. Grandpa dictating our images into a splintered photograph.

When he transferred his loyalty onto the white American paper, the soot black hair of his body began to fade. Swept the dark haunting man into shades of ash. The documents he was asked to sign bore the new definitions of his story, his allegiance to America, to a hostile West Coast.

He marked his name away from his family. Walked out of the chain and barbed wire fencing to deny his spirit soil. Blew the candle black. He quivered between day and night. Fought to preserve his body, the bodies of others, like insects already held in their air tight tomb denying them of a

language that would allow them
to cry.
Anything. In the end.

His handwriting looped, dodged the edges of the political
document, engraved his name into the government state-
ments. White line on top of white lines on top of white lines.
His signature became our scar tissue.

Grandpa became a military translator. A hybrid negotiator
fiddling with the toys of language. His hands lost touch
with the old ways, didn't move in ways that mirrored the
voices he knew. There was no marriage to tongue, no way to
bring the words and symbols together. Their friction created
the children that spilled out of Grandma.

Grandpa began speaking in slivered tongues, whipping
around the edges of his countries' broken translation. He
sliced his mouth under his double speaking. Telling too
much. With so many words his thoughts lost their color and
their country. His fingers smudged with the ink of calligraphy. Lips rough with the tones he learned as a child twisting against vowels and lateral language.

The dimensions of his speaking began to resemble flat
white paper and words housed in cages.

His sickness sat in the spit in his mouth.
Wet speaking, but far from water.
He formed new bodies and names. Grandma followed the
trail of his movements. Her sisters sat beside her parents.
They all sat with their hands tucked tight between their
legs. Waded in the stale air 'til the war was over. The sisters
began to speak in a hush. Quieter under the hush of men.

Silence that only displaced air. They guarded their voices licking at the backs of their teeth. Mouths that began to turn in, devour themselves.

The residue Grandma had collected on her hands at 17, turned to blood in the wake of Hiroshima. Singed fingers coaxed the babies out. She rolled them in the dirt surrounding Grandpa's feet. Bundled them in the crescent fold of her body. Bound their mouths from speaking too soon, that their skin would tell them all of the old stories. Didn't let them touch each other, the natural wandering towards same blood and bonestories.

Grandpa annunciated their names with ink pooling in the corners of his mouth. Turned them away from writing symbols that could help them find their way back to the little peach boy. My father, the glowing pit of my wonder.

I feel the scars he will not clean. Too tender, like the vein on a leaf. Rigid round words fall like marbles to cover the floor in his rolling rage.

Wet ceilings slump, the belly round, the belly big, inverted baby boy.
Ravens against a twilight sky.

I echo under the water, your name. This place cool with the scars traced under rocks. Inside the cleft of a hand. Grandpa, you tried to create a story with lady bug shirts and sweet sticky smiles. Made our painted cheeks stretch towards heaven.

Without you I would become a ghost.
With you I become a ghost.

I played the boy-game once, moved my body to recite the
rhythms of his voice. I stepped to his song, the light inside
his fingerprint.touch.myth.

This empty head, a moth to the flame. Your story.

Our story, a puzzle of song, lost against the skin of a word,
breathed deep beside a myth
of the peace of us.

Of tarnished wood memories.
Of bellies against the dunes.
Of dreams against the wandering of us.

Let's talk like children, I want to hear my father say. Let's find
another channel for our water rhythms. For swimming deep
and away to find a warm patch of stream. Let's begin again.

I hear my story, Grandpa.

TWENTY-ONE

I write my name on the inside of my legs with blood from my own lips. Pull the red ink from the places where I have bitten down for so long. Pressing bone towards bone out of habit. The brutal songs I sing to myself, to the children I have not had yet. The voice I can't hear is the one writing on the page. I am singing over my own voice.

There is a baby that sings from inside my body. My hands are like my mother's. Her hands are like mine. When I open up my mouth and tilt my head back I can feel her breathing. When she dies I wake up and begin to dream. It's the blaming that lets me live. Opens me. My dreams are telling me stories rubbed clean of what it means to be a man. Grandpa's wings down-turned, with his face buried in the earth, to reconcile the rupture of the family. The knots are loosening in the muscles of his children.

Grandma collects notes in her belly. The seat beside her is empty. Three pews back in the Baptist church she folds her hands in her lap and drops her chin to her purple collar and draws in a deep breath. I watch it lift her body. Her shoulders opening for a moment to let the air wrap into her stomach. When she exhales, her body returns to calm. Her wings wrapped over her lap. She raises her head and watches the piano keys disappear beneath skin at the front of the church. The visual divide of black and white coaxed by the pastor's daughter. Her hands light, her ribs close to her elbows. The notes washing the air in light.

I take the stones from the ashes in Hiroshima.
From the cracked rock in Tule Lake.

I have tried to track our story into the night with the soft
trail of your bread crumbs. I have filtered my offenses
through the eye of a needle. Cut the cloth before the hem,
tucked our secrets under the page. Write about the good
earth. Twirl the child's hair, the one I am scared to have.
Dream to have.

I build a fence to guard this home. Stitch a blanket against
your skin. I am your safety. You are my ventriloquist. I am
your loss.

Here, evenings fade and grow heavy with the rust in your
breath. Here I set fire to our compass rose. I imagine you
playing in the leaves of a humid summer night before you
were captured in a photograph. If there could have been a
before. You and I, forever inside and instead.

I pull the jagged edges of glass away from my skin and hold
them against the stones in my shoes. I build a body back
from these fractured myths and severed edges.

I am taking you home now, Grandpa. In breath and bone.

ACKNOWLEDGEMENTS

For, and to, the girls harnessed hot to the page. Kindra Kojima-Archie and Marisyn Camper-Wellman, whose stories we share in love and loss. For Anthony, our story that moves like water between brother and sister.

And to Doug Rice. For sharing the gift of language, and for the home I have found within it.

For a father, for a vein, for this path we have walked.

Thank you, to Janice Lee and Laura Vena. Who allowed me this breath and this space. Not without you both, and your beautiful gift of time.

An excerpt of this book has been previously published in *Gargoyle*.

OFFICIAL

CCM ◗

GET OUT OF JAIL
* VOUCHER *

- -

Tear this out.

Skip that social event.

It's okay.

You don't have to go if you don't want to. Pick up
the book you just bought. Open to the first page.
You'll thank us by the third paragraph.

If friends ask why you were a no-show, show them
this voucher.
You'll be fine.

- -

We're coping.

◗

CPSIA information can be obtained
at www.ICGtesting.com
Printed in the USA
FSOW02n2225230616
21925FS